FRAGILE INNOCENCE

A DARK MÉNAGE ROMANCE

DANI RENÉ

DEDICATION

To the girls who've met the monster.
To the women who've run from the monster.
Don't be afraid to speak up.
Don't let the monster win.
You are strong. You are strong. You are strong.

PROLOGUE

ELLA

EXPERIENCES DEFINE US.

Memories taunt us.

Dreams remind us.

Mine are dark, vicious, and demanding.

They've pulled and tugged at me, dragging me into crippling sadness.

Dreams, nightmares, images of what happened, of who I became.

The reality of my past has shaped me, molded me with its vicious claws.

When you're a child you're taught about the boogie man. The monster beneath your bed, the one hiding in the dark corner of your closet. But they're all just stories. They're tales made up to scare us.

Aren't they?

Not for me because I've met the monster. I came face-to-face with evil.

He, however, didn't lurk under my bed. Or in the recesses of my imagination.

And it was in the shroud of darkness that my soul was ripped from me. When all I knew was taken and I was left a shell of a girl.

I no longer believed in fairy tales.

The day I turned sixteen I learned the devil lurked in plain sight. And for two years, I had no way of escaping the clutches of the man I once trusted.

The scars are not external, but internal, and they haunt me when I close my eyes, leaving me crippled and damaged, and there's nothing I can do about it.

The memories of those years plague me on a daily basis. Like a horror movie playing out on a film reel. He violated me, stole my mind, and tainted every cell in my body. Wicked, vile images of when innocence was wretched from me violently, leaving me what he always called me—a broken girl.

I glance out the window and gaze at the stars twinkling in the night sky. As it always does when I'm lying in bed, the memory comes to me unbidden, unwanted, and it pains me as if I've cut myself and I'm bleeding out onto the pristine sheets.

Two weeks ago my life changed forever. When the girl

I was became a stranger. The birthday party my mother held for me was beautiful. She went all out with a cake, decorations, and all the kids from my grade were invited.

What made me happiest was the fact my stepfather was late home from work. I didn't want him there, but I could tell Mom was angry—even though she put on a smile for me.

I noticed the ongoing fights, the bruises, and marks on her arms and legs.

They got married two years after my father passed away and even though most kids would think their mother was replacing their dad, I didn't. She looked happy again, so I accepted him. Our new family.

He was amazing, friendly, and polite. When he took us on trips it felt like we were a real family, but something changed and it was only after the night of my birthday I realized what it was.

I was the problem.

It was my fault.

At least, that's what he tells me.

I had noticed the change in him in those weeks leading up to my birthday. He stopped hiding the way he looked at me. Or the way his hand would brush against me and I could feel his disgusting drunken glare on me, especially when I wore my gym shorts.

When he's been at the bar and comes home late, those are the days he hurts her. I don't know why she doesn't take me and leave. Even though I've mentioned it when he wasn't around, she laughed it off and told me to go do my homework, or that I didn't understand.

I did, though.

I hate when they have those arguments that turn into bruises and cuts. I hide in my room, curled up, trying to drown out the noise. After the first night, I made the promise to myself to get out.

Once I'm eighteen, I'll be free.

Rolling over, I glance out of my bedroom window. It's almost midnight. The full moon bathes me in its blue light and the stars twinkle in the inky sky. I used to love the dark, when everything is calm and quiet, but now it brings my nightmares. The sound of the lock has my ears pricking and I glance at the bedroom door, realizing too late that he's used his own key.

The door cracks and the large, formidable bulk watches me from the entrance of my bedroom. I want to scream, but no one will hear me. Mom passed out again. She told me she had a migraine, but I knew she was drunk.

I'm not stupid. The foul smelling liquor wafted from her like a sickly perfume.

I watch him walk into the room and shut the door

behind him. Only when the lock clicks does my body start trembling with fear. I want to be stronger, to fight back, but then he only hurts me more.

I used to hear stories about men like him, sick monsters who lurk in the dark waiting, watching.

My heart thunders in my chest and there's a lump in my throat threatening to choke me. My mouth opens, but no words come.

"Hello, little snowflake," he slurs, and I know why he didn't come home for dinner. The bar down the road must have been more inviting. He trudges toward me with a sway in his step. He's drunk again.

The man I used to trust, who used to care for me, is now the monster in my nightmares. He's the one who makes me cry.

"Answer me!" His gruff tone is enough to make me puke, but I swallow down the acidic bile and close my eyes.

"Please, don't do this again." My whimper annoys me because I want to sound stronger. I want to make sure he knows I hate him, but I'm afraid and the fear makes me weak.

"I'll fucking do what I want since your frigid bitch of a mother is passed out again. She doesn't let me touch her anymore, but you can make me happy." My stepfather turns to my window, tugging the blinds closed.

They say the strongest people are the ones who cry behind closed doors. Maybe that's me. Maybe I'm strong. The cotton sheet that was covering me gets ripped away and the cool breeze that sweeps over my body sends a shiver through me.

"My sweet girl, a fragile snowflake. I won't hurt you. I know you like to feel how much I love you. You're my temptation."

The sinister smirk that curls his cracked lips has revulsion crawling over my skin.

"Our little secret. You won't tell your mother because you know what you are. You're a whore. And you know she'll see you that way. She'll throw you out of this house so fast your head will spin. You'll never find someone to love you and you know why? Because you're broken and tainted. By me."

The demented chuckle echoes through my room and that's when the tears spill.

I'm strong. I'm strong. I'm strong. I chant in my head, hoping the words will one day ring true.

"Don't do this, please." Begging does nothing to stop him, but I ask anyway, hoping he'll see the error of his ways.

Rough, calloused hands stroke my legs and I want

to crawl inside myself. I want to hide from him, from my mother, from the world. "Open your fucking legs." Without waiting for me to move, he forces my thighs apart. His heavy bulk now presses my body into the mattress. My eyes are shut so tight I can see white behind my lids. "That's it, you feel that? Feel how happy you make me." His erection painfully presses against my core.

The pain is coming. The pain is coming. The pain is coming.

I get a small reprieve when he sits up to pull my shorts down along with my panties. Then suddenly I'm pinned down and he's driving into my body. His big, rough hand over my mouth muffles my scream at the searing pain that shoots through me as he takes my body. The same way he did the first night when he took the one thing I held onto—my innocence.

I am strong. I am strong. I am strong.

There are memories that bind us, memories that free us, and memories that destroy us.

I've been destroyed for too long.

I severed myself from friends, family, and even love because I couldn't be near anyone. I couldn't bring myself to smile and act like life was perfect when it so clearly wasn't. When my soul was carved out, held in the hand of a man I grew to love.

A man I grew to trust.

ONE

ELLA

MY ATTENTION IS DRAGGED FROM THE ROWS OF people queuing to the young man in front of me when he clears his throat. "Miss, can I see your passport, please?"

Handing over my little blue book, I watch the customs officer stare at my photo a little too long. It's always the same reaction. When I was growing up, it was my white-blond hair and gray eyes that used to capture unwanted attention. Now, my mocha color waves and the color contacts that give me a slightly amethyst shade to my irises garner me quizzical looks.

With my pale skin, it was easy to change my appearance when I ran. I didn't want him to find me. I did it to reinvent myself. My dark hair helped me forget the nickname he gave me. I was no longer *Snowflake.*

"Is something wrong?" I question, annoyed that he's been ogling my photo for far too long.

His head jolts up and he offers me a grin. "No, ma'am." Finally, he stamps the page and hands my passport back to me with a smile. "Enjoy your stay."

"Thank you," I respond with a tight smile and shove the damn thing into my bag. Luggage retrieval is easy since I don't have much. I never settled anywhere for too long and it made moving easy. Not getting attached to things, only needing the basics to survive.

On my eighteenth birthday, I ran as far away from him as I could, spending the first two years on the move, and I learned to never look back. I promised myself I'd never get caught, and now that I'm a thousands of miles away, I can finally breathe. But as much as freedom is within reach, I can't let my guard down. The man I ran from is a villain. I'll never be safe as long as he's still alive.

But running is second nature to me now. As long as I can keep two steps ahead, I'll be okay. At least, I pray I will. I've survived all this time, I'm sure I'll be able to keep doing it.

For so long, that's all I focused on.

Surviving.

Now, I hope a new city will give me a life and I'll be able to live.

When I landed my first job as an assistant to a real estate broker, it didn't take me long to figure out what I wanted to do with my life. My boss offered to pay for my studies in exchange for my long hours and a minimum of four years of servitude. It was a challenge, one I accepted. That's what brought me to one of Europe's busiest cities. London.

Now at twenty-four, I'm finally starting fresh in another city on the other side of the world where *he* can't find me. The job offer was one I couldn't refuse and when I packed my bags and walked out of the apartment in Brooklyn, a weight lifted off my shoulders.

Leaving the States has been a godsend because I'm far from what happened. At least, as far as my nightmares allow me to be because I still see *him* in my sleep. As soon as I close my eyes, he's there, haunting me.

Once my luggage is on the trolley, I glance around and find the arrivals terminal bustling with people. I hate airports. Emotion always seems to spill from every corner. It's too much for me to handle. I love traveling, but watching others' happiness when they're reunited with their families saddens me, knowing I've never had that, perhaps never will.

There are instances I wish there were someone eagerly waiting at the entrance for me. Someone I can run up to and throw my arms around. But I've become detached from others. Pushing rather than pulling.

My relationships, as short-lived as they've been over the years, have always ended up with me running for the hills. I keep my relationships with men strictly professional. It's been years since I've dated or allowed a man in my apartment, or even been to his. I don't do one-night stands. The initial reaction for me is fear rather than desire.

Pushing my way through the crowd, I take stock of where the exits are and head that way, hoping to find a cab rather than having to wait. Unexpectedly, heat sears me from the throng of people as if there's a flame licking its way up my body—from my black trainers, over my skintight jeans, up to my soft woolen jumper. Turning my head, I dart my gaze around, trying to find the pair of eyes burning a hole through me.

Normally, fear would be creeping up along my spine, but this is different. The stare pinning me to the spot is so much more. Turning to the large floor-to-ceiling windows that overlook the runway, I cast my gaze left and right.

When I find them, my heart stutters. I swear it stops.

I find the deep blue pools shimmering through the hordes. They're almost reflective in the sunlight streaming through the window behind him, effectively blinding me to their beauty. Swallowing the lump in my throat, my gaze drags itself over the man as he in turn watches me.

He regards me like a predator ready to pounce.

Deep in my gut, I realize I'd let him.

His immaculate suit is fitted to his body as if it was tailored specifically for him. I'm sure it was. A chiseled jaw is free of stubble. As if he's been molded from granite, his angular face is that of a Greek god. He stands taut and composed. Oozing confidence, sexuality, and dominance like a cologne that wafts around him, hypnotizing me.

His silky, jet-black hair is perfectly tousled, as if he's run his fingers through it, and my hands tingle, wanting to feel if it's as soft as it looks. One stray lock falls down the middle of his forehead and into his left eye. I haven't been ensnared by a man like this before, especially one like him—he looks like the ultimate specimen of the male species.

Unbidden desire coils deep in my gut, as if a noose is being tightened around my neck and he's the one controlling it—tugging me toward him.

From here, I'd say he's beautiful, perfect even. But then again, nobody's perfect.

His full lips lift marginally into a smirk—a dark, sinful smile.

A promise of something devious, decadent, and devilish.

Instead of fear gripping me, I feel a twinge of something I didn't think I could ever feel. Yearning. Shaking my head, I turn on my heel and hasten my way through the building. As I race farther from the stranger, my body cools and the pull toward him eases, allowing me to breathe.

As soon as my feet hit the sidewalk, a black cab pulls up. "Need a ride, love?" the driver questions with a thick British accent.

I offer a smile and nod. "Please, I'm heading to Knightsbridge."

He exits the cab and rounds to where I'm standing. With one hefty tug, he lugs my suitcase off the trolley and hauls it into the trunk.

"It will be forty quid from here. Is it a hotel you're going to?" His brogue is thick and I have to really pay attention to understand.

"I'm heading to this address." I hand him the piece of paper on which I jotted down my new address. He nods and I question further, "Oh, and the fare is forty pounds?" Feeling like a tourist, I watch his amused expression.

"Yeah, that's it. You'll get used to it in no time," he responds, speaking a little slower this time for me to catch the words. Nodding, I open the door and slip into the bench seat. My mind flits back to the stranger and I wonder who he is. Even though I know I shouldn't, I wonder what would happen if I saw him again.

Would he want to take me to dinner?

Perhaps a date?

"You here on holiday then?" the driver questions, distracting me from the unwarranted thoughts.

"No, I'm here for work actually. It's a short-term contract."

"Then I suppose a welcome is in order. I hope London treats you well." He offers a kind smile and as tense as I'm being alone with him in the car, I nod.

He turns the key and the engine roars to life. As we pull away from the sidewalk, I glance out of the window to find my hunter watching me as if he knows where I'm headed.

Would he find me? Or would the city swallow me?

Unlike Cinderella, I don't leave a slipper for him to find me.

Instead, I leave the dark prince in the dust. An excited smile plays on my lips and I wonder if I'll ever see him again.

Do I want to? Yes, perhaps I do.

TWO

CARTER

To say I'm both intrigued and frustrated is an understatement. I watch as her cab pulls away, then head to the town car waiting for me. It's parked in the pick-up section of the parking lot and I slip into the backseat. I nod at Baines, my driver of ten years. "Follow that cab, Baines. I want to see where she's headed."

He doesn't question me. Instead, he roars after the quickly disappearing vehicle. We're only three cars behind her, but I keep my eyes on the road. Swerving through London traffic is never a good idea, but right now, I don't care.

I feel like the goddamn prince chasing after a princess.

If Ben were here, he'd call me a stalker. I disagree. If there's something you want in life, there's nothing that can ever stop you from getting it. Why wait when life is so short?

I retrieve my phone from my pocket and type out a message to my assistant, letting her know I won't be in the office today. I should be focused on work and the upcoming charity event my father planned, but my mind is still on the woman with the incredibly unique eyes.

She's enamored me and I don't even know who she is.

"Sir, are you not going directly to see your father?"

Glancing up at Baines, I shake my head.

"Not yet," I respond, watching as we catch up to her. She doesn't know I'm behind her, so close, yet so far. "I'd like to know where this woman is staying before heading home."

"Do you know her?"

I chuckle. "No, Baines, she's… I don't know. I just saw her moments ago at the airport, but she's incredibly beautiful."

He laughs, the sound rich and heavy, smoky even. The man has known me most of my life. When I want something, I tend to get it.

"We'll head to the mansion soon. But first I need to collect paperwork from my father's office. I'm scheduled to meet him later, so we have time."

He doesn't respond as he follows her cab. I notice the closer we get to the city, we're headed for Knightsbridge.

Moments later, we're pulling up to one of the more elite apartment buildings. Strangely enough, I know who owns them. Smiling, I tap call on my phone. It only takes three rings before Bennett answers.

"What can I do for you, mate?"

"Who's the new woman you've got moving into the building in Knightsbridge?" I question my best friend. Bennett Ainsworth. Our friendship has moved from school, to college, and now that we both run successful companies of our own, not much has changed.

Even though Bennett's been involved in some shady deals when he worked for a security company, I'd trust him with my life.

Baines takes the road that winds toward the Hamilton Estate, while I ask my best friend for the information I need on my runaway princess.

"I've just followed her from the airport to your apartment building in Knightsbridge."

"You're such a fucking stalker, Cart," he responds

with amusement clear in his tone at my psychotic tendencies. Perhaps it was over the top following her, but the look she offered when she slid into the back seat of the cab was a challenge. *Find me if you can.*

"I'll have to check the log of new tenants. I have three new people arriving today."

"Get back to me later," I tell him. "After my meeting with my dad, I'll need some good news."

He sighs, knowing my relationship with my father is strained at the best of times. "I'll call you tonight. I'm heading into a meeting now."

I hang up before he says goodbye, knowing he'll curse me later for it.

I sit back, still annoyed at the pointless trip I made to the airport to collect my sister who wasn't even on the flight. She didn't even have the decency to let me know she missed it. The whimsical girl drives me insane. Sometimes I wonder if we're even related.

I'm about to put my phone away when it rings. Swiping the screen, I answer. "Hello, father."

"Carter, I'm running late. Meet me at four. Also, I spoke to your mother and told her I'm getting the private plane to fly your sister home because she needs to be here for the charity auction."

"I'll be there. I'm stopping at home to collect the documentation you asked for. I'm sure Kat will be back for the event. She knows how much it means to the family."

My family owns a chain of boutique hotels. We've had celebrities and royalty stay at our hotels and I'm about to take over the acquisition of new properties in different countries to expand the chain worldwide. My sister will take over the marketing, but if she doesn't behave herself, I have a feeling there may be a problem with her finally taking over from my mother.

"Well, let's hope she comes to her senses, because her immaturity has me wondering if she's ready to have this responsibility on her shoulders."

Nodding, I can't stop the heavy sigh that falls from my mouth, over the line to my dad.

"Yes, Father. I have to go. We've reached the house, I'll see you later."

"Yes." He never says goodbye, merely huffs and hangs up on me.

Baines pulls up to the high wrought iron gates and as they slide open gracefully, he heads up the driveway that will take us to the three-story mansion. It's a masterpiece of architecture and sometimes I still look at it in awe. It's ridiculously large and since I don't live here anymore, I hardly see it. When I turned twenty, I moved out and got my own apartment in the city, partly to get away from prying eyes, but also, I needed to have a space that was my own. Something I worked for and not something my parents gave me.

Climbing out of the car, I button my suit jacket and head toward the main door. Before I can knock, it slides open with ease and grace and I come face-to-face with my mother.

"Carter, come in. It's good to see you, darling."

"Mom. How are you?" I step inside the enormous foyer, then lean in and give my mother a kiss on the cheek. I get along better with her than I do with my father. As much as I love them both, she's always been more like me in most respects. Also, I look just like her with the Italian heritage strong in my blood, which has gifted me dark hair and my blue eyes.

"Are you staying for lunch?" She smiles with a hopeful expression on her perfect, unwrinkled face. She's in her mid-fifties, but you wouldn't say she is, not looking a day older than forty.

"No, I need to collect Dad's paperwork and then

I'm meeting him at Marcus' in Knightsbridge," I inform her, but I have a feeling she already knew that.

She walks along with me down the long hallway to the office and I know she's going to be fishing for information about a girl, so I wait for it.

"I hear Kat didn't make the flight?" Her question has my mind wandering back to the airport and the beautiful woman who captured my attention. It's as if she's ensnared me in a net. I know Bennett will get me her name and all the contact information I ask for.

Perhaps if he sees her, he'd be up for a session with us both indulging in her delicious curves.

"No, she didn't even bother to message me. It's ridiculous that I had to stand there for two hours." I stroll into the study that my father converted into an office. It's dark and dreary, like you'd imagine an old aristocrat's office to be, with a heavy cherry wood desk and bookshelves along two walls filled with old hardcover copies of classics and encyclopedias, even atlases from every continent. Most are first editions and are worth more than a night in one of our five-star hotels.

"Did you take out that lovely girl we met at the

polo match last week? She's a friend—" And there it is. Subtlety is not my mother's strong suit and when she starts with this, it doesn't stop until I'm walking out the door again.

"Mom, I know you mean well, but I'm not taking out any of your friends' daughters. Didn't we have this conversation? I want a woman who isn't privileged, someone who doesn't think the world revolves around her."

She steps forward and her hand on my arm stops me from rifling through my father's cabinet. When I turn to her, I find those familiar blue eyes on me.

We're so alike, whereas my sister is the spitting image of my father. My mother moved to London when she was a student, a young Italian girl attending Cambridge.

When she met my father, they didn't fall in love and live happily ever after. Their story is not your average romance. My grandfather, my mother's father, is a strict Catholic, and my father's family is Anglican. I don't really understand it, since I didn't grow up going to church, but apparently when my parents were younger it was important to marry someone of the same beliefs. It took my grandparents years to accept the relationship.

My mother has always been headstrong, stubborn, and adamant in what she wants. The saying goes that a boy's mother is the epitome of the woman he will seek once he's ready to marry. And that's true. Most of the girls my mother tries to set me up with are too pristine and entitled.

I don't want that.

I want someone who's going to challenge me and make me crawl on my knees to get into her pretty lace knickers, but once I'm there, she'll need to relinquish them to me because I'll own her. She'll allow me to take her where I want, when I want. Most women who are part of my family's social circle are dolls. They don't like their hair being messed, and they certainly don't enjoy me telling them what to do. And let's not talk about blindfolds, cuffs, or any sort of toys.

I want someone who likes it the way I do—rough, hard, and dirty. Who's going to take everything I give her and give back in return. And who, indeed, wouldn't mind a threesome with my best friend. Bennett and I have shared many women in our past. It's what we've always enjoyed. Most women are there for the experience and bragging rights to say they've had a threesome.

It's different for us, because I know deep down, if we found the right woman, Bennett and I would both claim and keep her as ours.

"I know, Carter, but I worry about you, darling. You're thirty-five and you're still single."

It's always the same conversation, every time I visit. My mother can't understand why I'm still alone, but what she doesn't realize is, I choose to be alone and rather focus on work.

The princesses I've been around all my life are hard work, which I don't need to deal with. They're clingy and needy, and the only time I want a woman needy is when my fingers are in her hot, wet pussy.

I prefer a strong woman who can hold her own. Who can take me as I am and not give in when they find out what an arsehole I am. Yes, I'm an arsehole, but not the pompous kind. I'm the kind that will rip your fucking knickers off and ram myself so deep inside you that you'd feel me for days, or weeks after and I'll do it wherever the fuck I please.

"Mother, I met someone, so if you stop pressuring me maybe I can focus on her." The lie slips from me so easily. Too easily. I grab the files from the drawer and turn to find my shocked mother staring at me like I'd just told her she's going to be a grandmother.

"You didn't tell me, Carter? How can you not tell your mother? This is news and I'm so happy. My boy makes me so happy." She grabs my face in her hands and plants a kiss on each cheek. At least she's happy. Now all I need to do is find the girl from the airport and make her mine.

I know where she lives. At least, I think she lives there. And tonight, I'll know for sure.

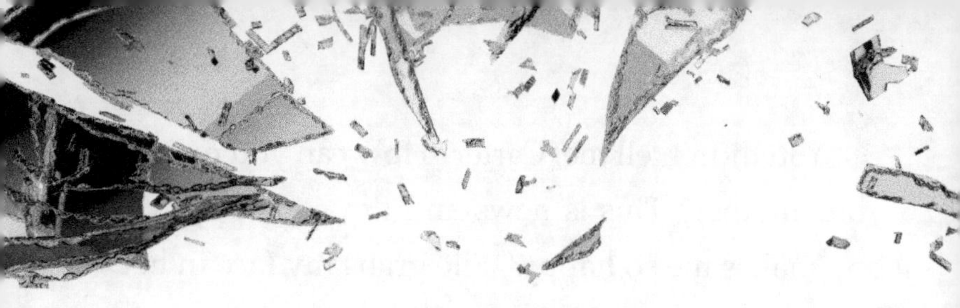

THREE

ELLA

THE APARTMENT THEY RENTED FOR ME IS IMMACULATE. In the middle of town—close to restaurants and stores—and furnished to perfection. I prefer simplicity to extravagance, and I would've never asked for something like this, but if they're paying, I might as well enjoy the luxury while I have it.

As soon as the cab dropped me off and I walked into my new home, I kicked off my shoes and changed into a pair of shorts and a tank top. Now as I step into the kitchen, I open the refrigerator and find it fully stocked. A buzzing sound distracts me from the amount of food I have and I turn to find a small white intercom on the wall near the entrance to the kitchen. Everything is open plan, but there's a counter that serves to cut off the living room from the rest of the area.

Pushing the white button, I lean in. "Hello?"

"Ms. Carmel, welcome to the building. I'm the security and doorman. If you need anything, just call me on the intercom. I'll be heading upstairs shortly to check in, but I wanted to let you know if you have any problems, let me know."

"Thank you and what do I call you?"

A deep chuckle crackles through the box on the wall. "My name is Alastair, but you can call me Al."

Biting my lip to keep from giggling at the reminder of a song, I nod.

"Okay, Al. Thank you." Hanging up, I turn to face the kitchen again and open the fridge. Grabbing a container of yogurt, I open the drawers, looking for cutlery. Once I've found a spoon, I make my way through to the living room.

The whole place is furnished in silver and steel and the sofa is plush black suede. There's a large fireplace on one wall with a flat screen above it. The rest of the walls are filled with bookshelves that have the classics, including one of my favorites. Jane Austen.

There's a small terrace off the living room, and as soon as I slide the door open the noise of the city assaults me, which I prefer because the silence sends fear rushing through me.

I take in the building design. It's shaped in a U with a park and swimming pool in the center. I remember seeing a sign for a gym and from my seventh-floor apartment I can see it down below. I love the architecture of the city. The historic buildings with the face brick or white washed walls intrigue me.

Tomorrow is my first day at work and I'm looking forward to it. Since I was a child I loved exploring homes and buildings with my father, who was an architect. I used to tag along with him to work and it's those times I remember with a smile and the ache in my chest doesn't hurt as much.

I was twelve when he died and my mother remarried the monster who haunts me to this day. Shaking my head of the thought, I watch the kids playing in the swimming pool below.

The sun is low in the sky and the jet lag hits me with full force. I yawn as sleepiness overtakes me. Since I stepped off the plane exhaustion has held me hostage. Thoughts of the airport assault me, as if I were being hunted by the predator. His blue eyes and sinful lips fill my mind, and I can't help clenching my thighs remembering the hunger they held.

Images of his perfectly tousled hair has my fingers itching to touch it. Desire heats my blood.

The feeling is foreign to me—to want a man. To crave his touch or kiss.

But with my hunter, I do. Even though I know I should erase him from my mind, the tug deep inside ignites the fire, warming me from the inside out. It seeps through my veins, making it feel as if my body is alight.

He would be the death of me. Luckily, I'll never see him again. The city is too big for a coincidence like that.

Spooning the last bit of fruity yogurt into my mouth, I lick my lips, but it's not the taste of the fruity flavor I'm relishing, it's the taste of his full lips I'm imagining.

Back in the kitchen, I dump the container and make my way into the bedroom. It's opulent and far too big for me. Pretty much the size of my old New York apartment.

The king-sized bed has midnight blue silk sheets and the carpet is an ash gray. A walk-in closet greets me on the right of the entrance, complete with four shoe racks, which I'm not sure how I'm going to fill since I don't own much.

Perhaps I can finally settle here, put down roots and have a normal life. The thought makes me laugh because I know I can never have that.

There's an en-suite bathroom, which has a shower big enough for two, or three, and a Jacuzzi bathtub that has some wicked thoughts running rampant through my mind. I picture my hunter undressing, dropping that immaculate white dress shirt on the tiles of my bathroom floor. His perfect muscles tense and tighten. I'm sure his shoulders are cut in the way women love.

A man like that is built for sin, sensual and erotic in every sense of the words.

I unzip my suitcase and pull out my clothes, dumping everything on the plush carpet. Piles and piles of material greet me. I should hang everything in the closet and tidy up, but there's nobody here to tell me what to do. Over the years, I've become accustomed to living alone. I love my independence and the freedom, even though at times I wonder what it would be like to come home to someone.

To have them wrap their arms around me and hold me tight. But then ugly images filter through the good ones and I remember why I'm alone.

It's no longer a choice, but a necessity.

With one more glance at the clothes on the floor I decide tomorrow is another day.

A wave of tiredness washes over me and I flop onto the bed. I need to get some sleep or I'll be useless tomorrow. Dreams of deep-blue eyes dance behind my eyelids, teasing and taunting.

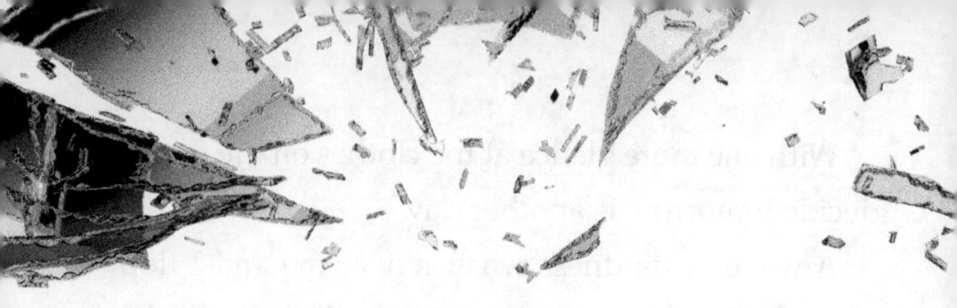

FOUR

CARTER

THE AFTERNOON PASSED BY TOO QUICKLY WITH THE lunch being as frustrating as I knew it would be. *How the fuck does my father expect me to be in three places at the same time?* Yes, we're expanding and I'm proud of that, but he needs to realize I'm one person and I can only do so much. The pressure is on and I hope to fuck Bennett can make sure I get the properties I want.

"Mr. Hamilton, your meeting with Ainsworth International has been moved to Friday," Brianna informs me as I stalk into the office.

Glancing at my assistant in frustration, I nod and respond, trying to keep calm. "Thank you, what time?"

"It's at midday, sir. Then you've got the property visit after with the agent. That is if you'd still like to do that? Since Friday afternoons are normally quiet

I don't think you'll be needed in the office."

"That's fine, block it out on my calendar. I'm possibly going to see Katherine after, so you may as well finish up at four on Friday."

She nods with a smile and continues typing on her computer. Heading into my office, I take a deep breath. Friday is D day. I hope I can convince my father I can do this and he can trust me with the future of Hamilton Enterprises.

Sliding into my overpriced office chair, I pull out my phone and scroll down to my best friend's number. Hitting call, I lift the phone to my ear.

He answers immediately. "Cart."

He's the only one who calls me that. Since I was a child everyone's always called me Carter.

"Bennett, what are you doing Friday night?"

"Your sister, if she gets her arse back here."

I cringe at his words. I know he's only joking because Kat will not go near him with a ten-foot pole, but he still tries. He has been since we were teenagers.

Groaning, I pinch the bridge of my nose in frustration, trying to get the image out of my head. "Do you have to say shit like that? I really don't want to know about you wanting to fuck my sister.

And you can keep dreaming, because she'll never let you near her."

He chuckles in response because he loves to rile me up, but it's not an image I'd like in my head while trying to concentrate on work. Or any other time for that matter.

"You tell me about your sex life all the time. I'm only returning the favor. Also, your sister would love to get a piece of me."

Spinning my chair, I look out of the floor-to-ceiling windows and take in the view of Tower Bridge and the Thames. The sun is about to set and as usual I'm still in the fucking office.

"I'm changing the subject because this conversation will force me to start drinking. Have you found my runaway princess? I need to find her, mate. She's fucking perfect." I'm gushing like a fucking teenager, but I need him to help me find her. We've been best friends for far too long and he knows me too well. There's never been a woman I wanted that I didn't get, and this one will be no different.

"Perfect?" He teases, "And that means you want to get inside her pants. I've had a look at our internal log. I'm guessing the woman you're talking about may be my new agent. She starts tomorrow."

It's my turn to laugh. I should have walked up to her and claimed those beautiful lips with mine. But, if he's right and she's about to start a job at Ainsworth International, I'll be seeing a lot more of her.

"Bennett, she's fucking exquisite." I get another deep chuckle from my best friend. He knows what I'm like. I give in to temptation more often than not and he's fueled my obsession dozens of times. When I lay eyes on a woman and want her, I'll do everything I can to get her. Some might call me a stalker, but if she wants it, is that still wrong?

I love beautiful things. I surround myself with only priceless items and women are no different. I want something that's going to entice and tempt me. And this woman did that with just one look.

"Are you telling me you'd want to perhaps play with her? Me and you?" Reading me like an open book, he's the one and only friend I'd ever do this shit with. And he knows it too.

"Me and you," I agree, no question about it. She'll be perfect between us.

"First, I need to find her. If she's going to be working for you, then you don't have to include yourself in this. I know you don't like mixing business with pleasure."

He laughs loudly at that. It's true. The man has had some beautiful women in and out of his office, but he's never succumbed to delving into the delights at work. Whereas I'm not as restrained. If there's a pert arse swaying around my office every day, there's no mistaking I'll have her bent over my desk pleading for more of my cock.

"I'm sure it's here. When she starts tomorrow on a short six-month contract. I'll be sure to let you know. I haven't met her yet, but if you can tell me what she looks like, I'll know."

I nod. "Long brown hair, the color of black coffee. She had the most intense amethyst eyes, almost purple. Her body is incredible, curves and legs for days with tits I could easily stick my dick between." Just talking about her has me solid steel behind my zipper. She won't know what hit her because I'll find her, and when I do, I'll make sure to enjoy every inch of her beautiful body.

"Then it sounds like we have ourselves a pretty new toy to play with. If she's as gorgeous as you say, I'll be dipping my fingers into that soon enough, Cart. As long as you're happy for me to join."

I nod, but I know he can't see me. It will be perfect. We'll enjoy her while she's here and when she leaves, we'll move on.

"Sounds good. Do you want to come over to my place tonight? My father bought me a bottle of Macallan Lalique 62-Year-Old Single Malt Whisky that needs to be opened." The old man gave me the almost fifty-thousand-dollar bottle as a gift of welcome into the hierarchy of the company, since he'll be stepping down and only have a say in board meetings. I'm pretty much running everything.

"It's Wednesday. I have an early morning meeting and then my new agent starting tomorrow and I need to have my head on straight. How about we crack it after the meeting on Friday? This lass is meant to be brilliant at her job, so I'm sure I'll be celebrating."

"We'll definitely be celebrating with her on Friday. Perhaps she'll be up for a few body shots. I can only imagine how delicious the Scotch will taste while dripping down her clit." We both guffaw at that and I'm sure the memory of our previous girl flits through his mind the same time it does mine.

The lights of the city below flicker on and I lean back, listening to his huff. My friend loves women.

Lots of them. That's why I'll never allow him near my sister, or she'll never allow him near her.

We've practically grown up together and he's hit on Kat ever since she grew a pair of tits. Even though she's turned him down numerous times over the years he's never given up. We're both in our mid-thirties and my baby sister—at least she is to me—is about to turn thirty.

Bennett has staying power; I'll give him that. But as soon as he knows we're about to have a woman between us, he moves on. Something about it tells me he's just messing with her, but then again, my best friend can be an arsehole when he wants it. I wonder if there'll ever be a woman who'll put him in his place and steal his heart.

"I need to go and finish up here before I head home. All the paperwork I had to do for this new girl is starting to get to me. I need a new assistant as well. Your sister wouldn't need a job, would she?"

"Jesus, Ainsworth, get off it. I'll see you Friday. My folks are off to Italy for their mini vacation. I'd like to be balls deep in our mystery woman by Friday night, so make it happen."

"Sometimes you can overreact about things, but if she's hot, I'll definitely want a piece of the action too," he quips back easily in his thick Northern accent.

"Fuck off, I do not overreact. When your cock is hard as fuck when you lay your eyes on her tomorrow, then you'll be apologizing to me in earnest," I bite back.

He chuckles before hanging up.

Shutting my computer off, I grab my phone and briefcase and head to the parking garage. My charcoal Aston Martin is one of my favorite possessions.

Sleek, sexy, and purrs when I touch her.

Soon enough that beautiful stranger will be mine.

And she'll purr when my fingers roam her curves.

FIVE

ELLA

THE TWENTY-STORY BUILDING THAT HOUSES MY new office is nothing like I was expecting it to be. Our offices in New York are modern with glass and steel, whereas this is the complete opposite. With deep auburns and bright reds that contrast each other, it gives off the illusion of a museum or art gallery perhaps. The property itself is old and I'm sure it holds history beyond my comprehension.

"Can I help you, love?" A soft female voice drags my attention to the large oak reception desk.

When I take in the woman, she looks to be the same age as me, late twenties, perhaps. She offers me a friendly smile and I recognize her accent as Scottish.

"Yes, my name is—"

"Ella Carmel?" My name rolls off her tongue in that thick brogue and I nod. "Nice to meet you, I'm

Elizabeth McKenzie. I'm pretty much the face of the company. Ainsworth International is one of the biggest real estate agencies in the UK," she informs me as she pushes up from the desk.

"Yes, I'm from the branched off New York office."

She nods and glances at the computer screen from her standing position and I notice she's slightly shorter than me.

"I'm supposed to take you through to meet Mr. Ainsworth." When she rounds the desk, I take in her black and red pencil skirt, which looks as if it's shimmering. Her white blouse is long-sleeved and fits her like a glove. Elegant. That's how I would describe her, reminding me of the film stars from the fifties. Her dark hair is pulled back in a severe bun and her makeup is flawless. Her dark eyes sparkle under the light of the chandelier. They're a rich brown that reminds me of dark chocolate.

I follow her farther into the building. "Is Mr. Ainsworth here every day?"

She presses the button for the elevator and nods with a quick glance at me. "He spends more time here than he does in his own home. He's lovely, though, friendly enough, but he has a way about him. Never seen him without a woman. He does love to wine and dine the ladies." She giggles and suddenly she seems younger than I thought she is.

"And how long have you worked here?" I continue my interrogation as the doors slide open and we step inside the empty car. Her finger pushes the button for the twentieth floor and I notice her nail polish is bright red, which matches the red in her skirt.

"I've been here for just under four years now. It's been good and I've learned a lot. They're paying for me to study, so I'm thankful I haven't had to fork out the money for my own tuition. The company is good to the staff. I suppose that's why we do so well. We come to work because we want to, not because we have to."

"That's great. My boss in New York was good to me for so long and I miss her, but I needed a change." The red number lights up and the doors glide open, giving me a view of my new office.

"Aye, that's good, darling. Come along, let's get you settled. You can call me Lizzie. Most of the people here do." She leads me to the two desks sitting side by side. Everything about this place makes me think I'm in a castle of some sort. The artwork on the walls is vintage and the antique vases that adorn the corners are ornate and beautiful. "This is your desk. Mr. Ainsworth's office is the one over there with the door closed. He's normally got it open, but if you see it shut, then you know he's in a meeting or his mate is over. You'll be meeting him tomorrow. Carter Hamilton. He owns half of the hotels in the UK. Or his dad does, but he's taking over the company and he'll be liaising with you on acquisitions," she rambles on and I can't help but feel slightly overwhelmed by it all.

"Lizzie, are you scaring Ms. Carmel away already?" A deep timbre rumbles through the office and straight down my spine. My eyes flit over to the man standing in the doorway that was closed only moments ago and I'm sure my mouth falls open as I gape at my new boss.

His hair is jet-black and his eyes are a bright green, reminding me of the fresh new leaves of a tree in spring. He appraises me with a slight smirk on his full lips and the heat of it scorches every inch of my skin.

"Mr. Ainsworth, I'll let you get on. I'm out for lunch later, but I've got one of the girls standing in for me."

He nods, but doesn't pay her any attention.

"See you later, love." She offers me with a smile and disappears from the office.

I haven't moved and neither has he. The air around us is thick with desire because the way he's looking at me is as if he's about to devour me.

"Ella Carmel." My name rolls from his tongue like silk caressing bare skin and it causes me to shiver. A twinge of lust teases over my skin, dotting it with chill bumps. It's the same feeling I got yesterday when I saw that stranger with the blue eyes.

"Mr. Ainsworth," I murmur a little too breathy for talking to your boss, but he doesn't act like he noticed. Instead, he steps forward, offering me his hand, and I slip mine in his.

His touch is warm, gentle, but commanding and I can't stop the ache between my legs.

Confusion settles over me. *How have I landed in a foreign country and suddenly turned into a wanton slut?* Somehow, he doesn't instill fear, though. There's something so much more coursing through my veins. Perhaps I'm not broken after all. Maybe I can be a normal woman.

"Call me Bennett, please." He smiles with the ease of a man used to getting his own way. Electricity swirls between us and all I can do is nod. "Welcome to London. I trust you'll enjoy the city and all the delights it has to offer." He leans in and his lips brush against my knuckles. Instead of cringing, like I normally do, I find myself wanting more. Needing him to hold on to my hand for longer.

"Yes, thank you." My words are a low whisper and I have to clear my throat to hide the need dripping from each syllable. When he lifts his eyes they pierce me, holding me hostage for a beat too long, but it's a look I'll gladly enjoy for as long as he gifts it.

"You've got a little bit of catching up to do." He releases my hand and suddenly I feel cold without his touch. "We've got a meeting tomorrow at midday. It's with Hamilton Enterprises here to meet about an acquisition. I want you to read through the file on your desk and familiarize yourself with them and their needs. Let's just say Carter Hamilton only wants the best and your job is to keep him happy."

"Is this your friend that Elizabeth mentioned?" I straighten my shoulders as my question hangs between us. There are times I come across as too direct, but I'd rather have that than to hide anything.

Most of my life I've held onto dark secrets that broke me. No more. When I finally ran away from home and left my mother with the monster, I vowed to never keep secrets again. And in my work, that's one of the most important traits I've found. Honesty and integrity.

He regards me with a small grin and nods. "Yes, the one and same." With that, he turns and stalks toward his office. Before he disappears from sight, he offers, "I'll leave you to get acquainted with the files on your desk, and your email is all set up. If you need anything, please let me know."

Rounding the desk, I turn on the computer and shove my bag into the small cabinet. My corner is comfortable and the furniture is positioned in such a way that I can see him when he steps out of his office, but he can't see me. The other desk next to mine is empty and I wonder who sits there.

As soon as my computer logs itself into the account, I find the mail app and open it. Within three seconds I have an email in my inbox from Mr. Ainsworth.

From: Bennett Ainsworth
To: Ella Carmel
Subject: Meeting — Midday Friday — Hamilton Enterprises

Dear Ella,

Firstly, welcome to Ainsworth International. I know you'll be an asset to our firm and I can't wait to see what you can do.

The first assignment will be with Mr. Hamilton. He's a difficult man to please, but if you can give him what he's looking for, your compensation will increase by 25%. I hope this pleases you.

If you ever have any issues at all, please come in and talk to me.

Kind regards
Bennett Ainsworth
Owner
Ainsworth International

Well, Bennett, I know my stuff, so your friend will get the best service he's ever had. Without being too confident, I can't help smiling. This is going to be easier than I thought. I know my shit and I'll make this the easiest acquisition he's ever seen. Hitting reply, I type out my response with a grin on my face.

From: Ella Carmel
To: Bennett Ainsworth
Subject: RE: Meeting – Midday Friday – Hamilton Enterprises

Dear Bennett,

Thank you. That's very kind of you. I'll make sure to have Mr. Hamilton smiling when we take him out to the venue after the meeting. And if he's not happy with that property, I'll do my utmost to find something he loves to ensure his satisfaction with our services.

Kind regards
Ella Carmel
Real Estate Broker
Ainsworth International

Sitting back, I open the folder and start my research on my newest client. Hamilton Enterprises is definitely going to bring in the cash from the figures which shows their income and what they're looking to spend. No wonder Bennett wants me to bend over backward for Carter Hamilton. I thought it may just be because they're friends, but this contract is worth millions.

Getting lost in the information, I make notes in the spiral-bound book I found in my drawer. I respond to emails as they come in. Glancing at the time, I notice it's just hit midday. Without a break, I don't notice I'm starving when I sit back to read through my documentation.

It's only when I finish the last few notes do I notice my stomach is protesting. But I can't fight the excitement that ripples through me at this opportunity. It's been a long while since I felt at ease, and being here in these offices gives me that sense of calm.

I'm not sure if it's Bennett, or if it's the fact I'm so far from my past, but I find my mind is clear for the first time in years. Eight long years of nightmares and fear, but I've survived.

I am strong. I am strong. I am strong.

"You do realize you can take a break, right?" My boss's deep voice comes from in front of me, startling me, and when I snap my gaze up, I realize I've been sitting here reading for almost five hours.

"I didn't even notice how much time had passed,"

I confess.

"I'm heading out for a late afternoon meeting. You're welcome to pack up and head home. No working late in this office. I actually prefer you to get that beauty sleep you don't need." His mouth lifts.

A smirk. Devilish. Sexy.

"Thank you, Mr. Ains—" Realizing my mistake, I nod. "Bennett."

He acknowledges me a moment longer, then disappears toward the elevators, leaving me staring at his retreating broad shoulders. He's utterly beautiful. Like the man from the airport. Confident and cocky, but alluring and intriguing.

Sighing, I pack the folder, notebook, and my printouts about Hamilton International into my bag and turn off the computer. I head out with my mind on my meeting tomorrow, happiness bubbling in my stomach. It's a foreign feeling. But I think I can get used to it.

SIX

CARTER

MY PHONE RINGING DRAGS MY ATTENTION FROM the document I'm reading for today's meeting and when I pick it up, I sit back and slide my finger over the screen. "Bennett, are you missing me? Can't wait till midday to see my handsome face?"

He chuckles at my greeting. "Fuck off. I was calling to talk to you about my newest member of staff."

My interest is piqued at this. My best friend told me he'd call me as soon as he could, but he was kept busy all day in meetings. He did, however, send me a photo of the woman in question and it is indeed my princess. I wanted to get more information from Bennett last night, but he had a loud of shit to deal with. I didn't ask. "Okay?" My voice is wary when I respond.

"I'm definitely going to be getting some of that. She's fucking beautiful." This has me laughing out loud. I've known him my whole life, but I've never heard him refer to a woman as beautiful. It's been hot, sexy, fuckable, but never beautiful.

"Yeah? And do you think she's going to allow us in?"

He huffs at my question but responds with confidence. "She better because I'm hard just from shaking her hand. You were right. She's exquisite. I thought about her last night, mate. I haven't been so entranced by a woman in a long while."

"Jesus, calm down, I really don't want to know if your dick is hard right now." He sighs and that has me more alert than anything. Bennett is your typical manwhore. He fucks them and before they've come down from the high he's out the door.

"Her eyes are the color of an amethyst, Cart. It's unique, just like her. I haven't seen anything like it. She's got an accent that I'd bet would sound amazing when she comes all over our dicks."

I can't help laughing at my best friend. "Well, I look forward to seeing her up close and as personal as you have. And don't you go fucking around with her and not telling me. I'll have your balls, mate."

"We'll be sharing this woman one way or another. I want her. And I know you do too." His voice drops at the statement and my mind wanders back to the last night we shared someone in the most intense moment we've ever had. That was incredible. We've done it a few times before and every time it's been an explosive experience.

"You've made my morning. I'll see you later?" I listen to him chuckling at that. I thought about her last night, while I stroked my dick, imagining her beautiful lips wrapped around the base as I fed her my hard cock. I can't remember a time I came so hard.

His voice drags me from the memory as he once again jokes. "We may want her to take us both, but ultimately it's her choice. However, I have a feeling if she does choose, it will be me."

"Quit dreaming, fucker," I retort, but he knows I'm not serious. Would this girl be the one who finally brings us both to our knees? He's right, it is her choice, but we'll make it so irresistible that she can't say no.

As we say our goodbyes, I hang up and find myself smiling. I felt unsettled last night. The idea of a woman who seemed to claim me as much as

I want to claim her is new to me. I've never come across this feeling, and I'm sure my mother will tell me it's fate or some shit. Whatever it is, I want more of it.

Walking into Ainsworth International, I glance at Elizabeth. Her unfading smile is something I've gotten used to over the years and even now, when she glances up, her face beams with a wide grin.

"Hello, love. How are you today?" I quip, earning me a blush. Her smooth, pale skin is bright red as she regards me with those big brown eyes.

"I'm all right. Thank you, Mr. Hamilton." Her lilt is adorable, and I nod as I pass her desk.

At the lift, I push the button and wait for the doors to open and accept me into their depths. I'm looking forward to meeting this new real estate broker who's meant to be an expert at what she does.

If she can please me, I'll beat my best friend into her knickers and I bet Bennett would give me shit for it. I chuckle at the thought of my best friend falling for someone. Stepping into the waiting car,

I press the red number twenty. My phone beeping alerts me of a text message and when I glance at it, I find a message from my father wishing me luck.

It must be difficult allowing someone else to take over something you've spent your life working on, but I'm his son. He should trust me.

My parents' relationship hasn't been smooth sailing and the fact he's taken her home to Italy is a good sign. As much as they love us, Kat and me, there's not so much love between the two of them anymore.

But they need time off from the business and the distractions, and I need the quiet. I quickly respond and slip my phone back into the pocket of my trousers.

The doors slide open and I step out, turning right. As my gaze lifts to the desks outside Bennett's office, I'm halted in my tracks. As if I've slammed into a wall. It is her indeed.

My world spins on its axis when I'm met with those eyes.

"Carter."

My gaze gets dragged to my friend, but my feet don't move. I can feel her eyes on me. They're scorching me. Burning into my skin as she takes me in, from head to toe.

"Bennett." Forcing myself forward, I reach out and shake his hand. My eyes haven't left the woman sitting at the dark cherry wood desk.

"This is Ella, the newest asset to Ainsworth International, and she's here to make sure you're happy with the service. I have given her your account to handle, so anything you need, she's your girl. Ella, this is Carter Hamilton."

She pushes up from the desk and I can now fully take her in.

My hungry gaze trails from her long mocha waves, to those gemstone eyes—that hold me hostage for a moment too long—down to the sleeveless silk blouse she's wearing. The buttons just about close over her cleavage and I have to stifle a groan. Her hourglass figure is exceptional and her hips are hugged by a pair of black pants that have my dick throbbing.

Every inch of her is perfect. From her body to those pretty red heels on her feet, and I know I'm so fucked. So incredibly fucking fucked because this woman is going to be my end.

"Nice to meet you, Mr. Hamilton." Her voice is like a smooth whisky and I feel the burn all the way down my throat. I'll take a shot of her neat any day.

"The pleasure is all mine, Ella." I offer her a smile and the blush on her cheeks has me biting my tongue to keep from groaning out loud. If I wasn't hard earlier, I'm fucking steel right now. Leaning in, I brush my lips over the top of her hand and I don't miss the sweet tremble that wracks her body. She wants me, and my God, I want her—under me, on top of me, against me. "Bennett, can I talk to you in private before the meeting?" I question but don't take my eyes off her. "Excuse us for a minute, Ella." Shoving my best friend into his office, I shut the door.

"What the fuck was that?" Confusion is spread over his face as he regards me with narrowed eyes.

Pointing to the door, I hiss my response. "She's… Fuck, Bennett. I want this."

"We'll ensure she's ours," he tells me easily, confidently.

Inhaling a deep breath, I look at my best friend. His bright green eyes are almost luminous with mischief and I nod.

"I've heard from my contact in New York she's amazing at what she does. As long as you don't break her heart, because I'd like to keep this one."

He shrugs nonchalantly and walks over to his desk.

"Bennett, I want her."

He glances up and pins me with a serious glare and I think he's about to tell me to fuck off when he shocks the shit out of me. "Well, then go get her."

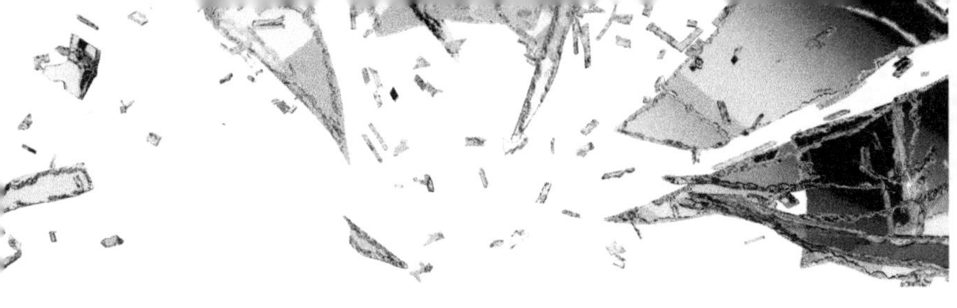

SEVEN

ELLA

Y BODY WAS ALIGHT WITH AN ACHE LOW IN my stomach. Both men commanded my attention. They held the air in the room hostage while they appraised me. My blood heated to the point of pain when I laid eyes on him. I'd found words were lost to me. There wasn't anything I could say to sound intelligent.

When I first saw Carter at the airport, I felt it, but with both of them near me, I'm helpless to the pull they have over me. My fear is gone and I feel almost normal.

So far both men have rendered me speechless. A dumbstruck teenager with a crush on two of the hottest boys in school. Sadly, I never got that far. School was an escape from hell. But each afternoon I returned, it was as if I'd walked into Satan's home.

Carter's hungry gaze roved over me, like most

men I've come across, but the difference was, I wanted his eyes on me. His stare pinned me in place as if he were about to eat me. *My God, I'd love for him to eat me.*

Shaking the dirty thoughts from my head, I glance at Bennett's office door. They've been in there for ten minutes and my curiosity goads me to knock on the door.

Both men ooze sex like it's part of their DNA, although they're both very different, one with sapphire eyes, the color of a gemstone, and the other with eyes the color of leaves in spring.

Bennett is not as refined as Carter, but they both have women dropping their panties easily and I think they're used to getting their own way. I haven't been this attracted to anyone in a long while. Or ever. I've always steered clear of anyone who showed sexual interest in me because fear held me back.

I'm tainted, broken beyond repair, but something about these men seems to drag me from my hidden anguish and sends me spiraling with need. A yearning that's so foreign to me, yet perfectly acceptable for any other female. The ding of the elevator drags my attention from the thick wooden door and I find Elizabeth walking toward the meeting room pushing a trolley of coffee and snacks.

"Did you meet him then?" she questions in her thick brogue.

"Yes, he's..." I can't find the word to describe Carter. *Handsome? Sexy? Drop dead gorgeous?*

"He's got your eye then, lassie?" She giggles and continues into the room, which is furnished with an enormous oak table and twelve chairs. I rush in behind her and shut the door.

"Do you know much about him?" My voice drops to a whisper and I can't help smiling like a teenager.

Is this what it's like to have a crush?

To want a man rather than fear him?

"He's one of the richest men in London. He's thirty-five and still single. Hasn't been in a relationship for about ten years now at least. That's the story going around. Not sure what happened when he was younger, but I've heard gossip from the girls who've worked with him before." She watches me, gauging my reaction. Before I can respond the door opens with a soft whoosh and I'm assaulted by two different scents of cologne that cloak me in their masculinity.

They're both tall, with broad shoulders, and they seem to loom over my five-foot-six frame.

"You two enjoying your banter?" Bennett's gaze settles on me then on Elizabeth and he offers her a small smile. The blush that pinks her cheeks doesn't go unnoticed and I wonder if there's something between them.

"I was helping set up. Are we ready?" I question. My gaze flits between them and they nod while strolling into the room and suddenly the large area feels stifling.

Once the door closes and it's only the three of us, I slip into a chair at the head of the table and wait for them to get seated. Carter settles in beside me and my skin prickles at his nearness. The heat emanating from him warms me and the panic that normally sets in doesn't threaten to choke me as it always does.

"Ella, as you would have seen in the file I gave you, Carter is taking over from his father and will be working with you on all acquisitions. He's the go-to for anything related to new properties and I have a list of areas he'd like to invest in. Also, I'd like you to do some research on the different countries where we can expand. Since you know the US quite well, I'd like a report first thing in the morning for New York. I was telling Mr. Hamilton that you're an expert."

Turning to the blue-eyed man beside me, I meet his gaze as it settles on mine and his mouth quirks into a sinful grin. There's an elicit promise in his eyes and it has me wondering what it could be. If he'd show me when we're alone.

"I guess you could say I'm an expert. I know New York like the back of my hand. Having lived there for four years, I studied the areas and I can find the hidden spots that most tourists prefer because it's not as busy as Manhattan itself. I can certainly say I can give you exactly what you need." As soon as the words tumble from my mouth, I stop, realizing how that sounded. Deep blue flecks shimmer with amusement, like a darkening ocean in the dim light of an evening sky.

"I have no doubt you can, Ms. Carmel. I certainly would love to see how you perform under pressure, because let me assure you, I'm not an easy man to please." There's so much more hidden in those few words and I can't stop a smile from creeping onto my lips.

Flirting. It's so new, so foreign, but with him it

comes easy.

My nipples harden under the intensity of his stare and I squeeze my thighs together. The ache that flared to life at the airport when I first laid my eyes on him is back and it's burning me like a live flame. Hot and torturous, and I want him to extinguish it.

"Great, now that we got that out of the way, let's move on to the venue." Bennett's voice cuts through the desire swirling in the air between us, but nothing can diminish the yearning that has my heart racing for the man on my left.

He shifts to grab the cup of coffee on the table and the material of his suit brushes lightly against my skin, sending a spark—elicit and wicked—through me.

Lifting the coffee to his mouth, I cut a quick glance as he sips the creamy liquid. The foam that tops his coffee sticks to his lip and when his tongue darts out to lick it off I find myself chewing on my lower lip, trying to keep the moan from falling from my lips.

The response of my body to him must be obvious and my cheeks heat in embarrassment.

You're a tainted, broken girl.

His voice screams at me through all the need and

desire. And once again I'm brought back to the truth of what I am. The monster from my nightmares ensures I never forget who I am. What I am.

"Ella?" Bennett's voice drags my attention back to him where he's seated on my right. *Shit*. There's amusement dancing across his handsome features and I realize he must have caught me watching his friend.

"Yes, sorry. I think jet lag is catching up to me," I offer with a nervous grin.

"That's okay, I understand. I was telling Carter you'd accompany him to the hotel. Since you're familiar with architecture, I want you both to work closely on this deal. The owner is ready to sign; he just wants the original façade kept as is."

I nod. That's easy. I've dealt with owners who find it difficult giving up their buildings.

"Yes, sure."

"And then you can finish for the day. I'm sure Mr. Hamilton won't mind dropping you off at your apartment, will you, Carter?" His gaze flits over to Carter and I follow Bennett's gaze.

The man next to me straightens and sets his cup down. "Of course. I would be happy to escort you home. Are you ready?" Inquisitive eyes land on me and I nod.

Every time he looks at me I lose all power of speech, which is ridiculous. The effect he has on me is surreal, and I find that fighting it will only hurt, so I let the feeling wash over me and enjoy the flurry in my stomach. *Just like a teenage girl.*

"Yes, I just need to grab my purse and the file with the information of the hotel. Maybe we can get the owner to sign today." I push up from my chair and glance at my boss, then my client.

"Perfect." Bennett's voice is light, not the deep rumble from earlier, and as both men stand up and follow me out of the meeting room I'm scorched by their heated gazes.

EIGHT

CARTER

THE VIEW I HAVE AS I FOLLOW HER OUT OF THE meeting room is beyond incredible. I can't help but watch the sway of her hips, which hardens my cock painfully. Imagining her bent over while I pound into her from behind runs through my mind. To hear that sexy accent calling out my name as she comes hard all over my dick while it's buried deep inside her tight body would be exquisite.

Visions of her in nothing but lace entrance me. Her creamy skin would look exquisite in the soft black material. When she leans down to grab her purse, my throat dries and my hands fist at my sides.

"She's definitely easy on the eye." Bennett's voice in my ear cuts through the haze.

"Don't go scaring her off before we've even got to the second step," I hiss under my breath. I know

I agreed to share her, but for some reason, I don't know if she'll go for it. Her body language, the tension in her shoulders are telltale signs that she's nervous around us.

He glances at me with curiosity. My possessiveness is enough to have him stepping back. Shit, this woman is already fucking with my head.

"Ready." Her sweet voice comes filtering through our standoff.

I need to calm the fuck down. He knows there are integral steps to having a woman pliable between us. I take the first tow, and he takes the last.

"Let's go, Ms. Carmel. Bennett, I'll see you later." Without waiting for a reply, I walk out toward the lift and push the call button. When she steps beside me, I inhale deeply as the scent of her perfume fills the air around us. A soft scent of orange blossom has my mouth watering and I wonder if she tastes as sweet as she smells.

The lift arrives after a moment and I wait for her to enter first then follow.

Pressing the ground floor button, I watch the steel doors close.

Being alone in a confined space with her has every inch of my body alert and my hands itch to touch her. To feel how silky her skin is. I'd love to fist her hair and thrust my cock between those perfect arse cheeks.

Clearing my throat to hide the groan, I turn to her. "Do you enjoy doing this? Selling and buying properties?"

She smiles and my heart kicks so hard against my ribs it feels as if it's trying to break out of my chest.

"I do. I found an early love for buildings and architecture. Drawing wasn't a passion, but history was. The story the walls of an old building hold is fascinating. As soon as I finished school, an opportunity arose for me to learn more about the profession, buying and selling, as well as appraising."

The reverence with which she talks about her work is intriguing.

Not only is she beautiful and sexy, but incredibly intelligent.

"Who taught you about architecture?" My question immediately brings sadness over her perfect features and her smile falters.

"My father." She drops her voice as if he'll hear her talking about him.

"And where is he now?" As soon as I ask I feel guilty because tears shimmer in those amethyst eyes. They glisten as if there's a flame behind them and I realize that no jewel could sparkle and capture me the way her eyes do.

"He's... Uhm..." She straightens and lifts her chin. "He passed away when I was twelve." Her voice cracks and I have the urge to hold her. But I don't. I stand there like the cold-hearted bastard I am. The one who doesn't want love, only a good fuck.

"I'm sorry." My response is automatic, but she offers a slight nod. The doors slide open and I step out first, forgetting my manners. I stop and turn. My fingers find the small of her back and she flinches. She's not used to being touched. *Well, too bad, sweet thing, you'll be used to being touched, kissed, and fucked when we're done with you. And you're going to love every fucking second.*

I flash a smile at Lizzie when we pass the reception desk. She's a lovely girl and I know she's got eyes for her boss. Who am I kidding, the whole female population is blinded by my best friend.

When we step onto the pavement, I murmur, "Over here, love." Leading her over to the waiting car, I open the door. While she slips into the bench seat I take in an eyeful of her arse and decide my favorite view is her bent over in front of me.

I need to fuck her to get rid of this ache because it's the only way I'll be able to work with her. There's no other option because a hard-on every time I'm around her is going to be unpleasant.

Once I've shut the door I glance over at her. "You can tell Baines the address."

She leans forward and gives him an address of the hotel not far from where one of our other properties is. My father must have chosen this one for a reason.

Her body is so close to mine I can feel the current racing between us. There's a nervous edge to her. Glancing at my driver in the rear-view mirror, I give him a nod. The partition rises and we're alone.

"I'm sorry if I upset you earlier. I didn't mean to pry. My conversation skills clearly aren't up to par." I offer a smile and she gives me a brilliant one in return.

"It's okay. I just don't talk about him much because I don't have any friends who knew me when I was younger."

I can't help frowning at her explanation. *How do you not know anyone from your childhood?*

"What do you mean? You don't have any childhood friends?"

"No, I came out here alone. When I left home at eighteen, my past stayed behind. There wasn't anyone who would… I mean, there's just nobody in my life right now." She stumbles over her words and I realize there's a lot more to this intriguing beauty and I want to peel back layer by layer until I've found out what lies beneath the exquisite exterior.

"It's such a foreign concept to me. I've always been surrounded by family and people who called themselves friends, but weren't. The thought of being alone scares me." I don't know why I'm confessing my deepest fears to this woman. I don't want to lay myself bare in front of her. She's not here forever, not my forever. Even though one day I'd like that, I know my past choices aren't as pristine as I'd like people to think.

I've never been a good man. My actions were merely paid off by my father—hundreds and thousands of pounds. When you have money like we do, everything you do can be swept under the rug. Even when my uncle—my father's brother— went down the slippery slope of addiction, the famous Mr. Hamilton stepped up and paid for him to go to rehab in one of the most expensive centers.

My past is riddled with those mistakes. Each one of them worse than the other. From women, to drugs, I did it all. But it's when I truly fucked up, when I hit rock bottom did I realize I needed to pull myself together. My father forced me to return to London, and it welcomed me happily.

When I chose to study in America, Dad supported me. I was the youngest student at Yale, and because my parents couldn't leave the family business, I traveled with my uncle as my guardian. He was there for me to a certain extent, but he was also the reason my life fell apart.

Bennett was the only friend who stuck around when we left. He followed me to the US and we partied like rock stars, and when I was dragged back to London, he followed too and he made a name for himself. First working for a security company before finding his footing in real estate.

Even though I only spent a short time in America, I miss it. If I didn't fuck up the way I did, I think I'd still be there.

"I guess we all have different lives. We all have those monsters we hide in the dark and they seem to materialize when we're alone." Her words are filled with truth and secrets all rolled into one and when I glance over at her again there's something hiding behind that mask she wears.

I've never been one for games, but I'd like to play hers. To uncover what she's got hidden in those amethyst eyes.

NINE

ELLA

THE DRIVE IS SILENT AFTER MY CONFESSION AND I have the feeling he felt guilty about bringing it up. As the car slows, I glance out the window and find the hotel we've come to see. A historic castle type building that looks as if it's been standing for centuries and I suppose it has.

My gaze flits over to Carter and I watch his expression change from moody and dark to friendly. There's something about him that has me intrigued, a deeper layer that I want to uncover. To break through that serious façade and see what lies beneath.

Before I can say anything, the door opens and I glance at his driver, Baines, as he holds a hand out for me. Slipping mine in his, I step out of the vehicle and take in the countryside. The air is clean and I can't stop myself from taking a deep breath, savoring the smell of freshly cut grass. Even though we're in the middle of autumn, it's warm out and I relish the heat of the sun.

"You seem to enjoy the sunshine." His tone is like velvet slowly sweeping across my skin and the heat of his breath fans over my neck, causing a shiver to race through me. Instead of revulsion, desire swirls through me, setting my body on fire.

"I do." Turning my head, I find his face inches from mine. Liquid heat shimmers as he regards me. It's entrancing and I can't stop staring at him. It's as if his eyes are glistening with desire before me.

"Good, I hope you'll find many more things to enjoy while you're here." His mouth quirks and those sparkling orbs darken with something that has my core clenching. His hand finds my lower back and we head into the foyer of the historic building. His touch is tender, but there's a commanding sensuality about the way he guides me with the lightest of brushes against the soft material of my blouse.

We find a man at the reception desk, who looks up as we near the counter. He glances between Carter and me with a scowl. This isn't going to be as easy as I thought.

"Hello, we're here to have a look at the building for Hamilton Enterprises," I offer a small smile, but I'm met with another harsh glare.

"I know who you are, lady. You can go ahead. Mr. Bishop isn't here to show you around, so you'll have to take the tour alone."

Nodding, I offer another smile and turn to the hallway on the right of the reception desk.

"That went well." Carter's voice beside me is a low murmur and I can't help giggling.

I regard him and find a grin cracked on his handsome face. When you see this man serious, it's astounding at how handsome he is, but when he smiles, my heart stops.

"It seems as if they don't like you as much as Bennett said. I suppose if you're buying their livelihood to demolish it, they'd be concerned."

He stops abruptly. When I turn to look at him I find emotion something akin to annoyance swimming across his features.

"Is that what you think of me? That I'm purchasing this building to either knock it down or lay off these people?" His body is positively vibrating with frustration. I know anger when I see it, and this right here isn't far from it.

"Carter... Mr. Hamilton, I really didn't mean it that way. All I meant was that when you've spent your life working for something, to have someone walk in and change everything you've ever known, it's difficult. It changes you." As I finish I realize I'm no longer talking about the hotel but confessing more about me than I ever wanted anyone to ever know.

"I know. I mean, I'm sorry. I shouldn't have gotten angry. It's just difficult. People see us walk in with our money and they think we're here to throw our weight around, when in actual fact we're trying to save the dwindling income of these people." His explanation catches me off guard. From what I've read about Hamilton Enterprises is that they only cater to the elite.

"But, your hotel chain, it's only—"

"It's there for the rich so we can pay the staff wages and to give the original owners money for them to retire. We only buy property from people who can't afford to run the businesses anymore." A smile cracks his serious demeanor. "Come on, let's look around, Ms. Carmel." With a wink, he guides me once again with a light touch.

The hotel is incredible and after numerous

hallways and way too many flights of stairs, I'm standing at a window that overlooks the garden. The greenery is discolored, no longer green, but rich oranges, reds, and browns. The grounds on which this hotel is built are incredible. There's a small hill that leads to a forest and I wonder if kids enjoy rolling down into the lush lawn that I'm sure fills that section in the height of summer.

"Penny for your thoughts?"

Pivoting, I find the handsome man who's been great company the last hour we've spent roaming the halls.

"I was just looking at the grounds. They're incredible." I point to the window and when he joins me the attraction between us smolders. There's an obvious magnetism, but I wonder if he feels it too.

"Can I take you to dinner tonight?" The question comes out of nowhere, and my eyes flit over to him. His face is lit up with excitement. There's kindness dancing on his features. I want to say yes. But, can I be normal? Maybe I can let go of my pain, my past, and my nightmares.

"Sure. Just so you know, I don't mix business with pleasure." My sassy mouth takes over and the smirk that curls his lips has me wondering if he'd kiss me.

"Somehow, I have a feeling you don't really know what pleasure is, *Princess*."

I fully face him, our bodies close, and I can feel the soft material of his dress shirt against my blouse. My nipples harden against the lace of my bra and my heart thuds against my rib cage.

"Princess?" I giggle. "What's that supposed to mean?"

"Well, you ensnared me, then ran off at the airport. You left me to find you, only, you didn't bother leaving behind one of your Louboutins." His grin widens, the crinkling at the corner of his eyes making him look even younger than he is.

"I don't just leave my shoes lying around for anyone, you know. There's no telling who's a frog and who's the prince." I can't help the carefree laugh that falls from my lips.

He reaches out and strokes his knuckles over my cheek. Fire follows the trail of his touch as if he'd struck a match and held it against me. A shiver runs down my spine and straight to my black lace panties.

"There's so much tension radiating from you right now I could probably light the hotel with the energy. Don't you ever let go?" His whispered words send a jolt to my chest.

Let go, Snowflake. Take me, little one.

A scent of cigars and whisky filters through the room, attacking my nose. *He's here.* He can't be. I know this, but the hallucinations never stop. It's as if he follows me everywhere I go.

My heart leaps into my throat and my mouth opens, but no words come out. He doesn't know how much I hold onto. The thought of letting go is like me leaping off the roof. I may as well be dead. I can't find the appropriate response to explain my life to this man. Even though I want to let go, I'm not sure I can. "Look, Carter—"

"Shh…" he whispers and reaches up to place a finger on my lips, which causes a tingle to trickle its way gently through every nerve in my body. "If there's one thing you'll learn about me, Ms. Carmel, I never take no for an answer. I'm also an expert at making sure you relinquish anything you're scared of. Lastly, make no mistake, I don't make anyone do anything they don't want to, but I guarantee you'll release whatever you're holding onto, beautiful." He leans in and I feel the heat of his lips on my ear. "I promise. You're a temptation in the dark, Ella."

His voice drops on my name, caressing it, savoring it.

And you seem to be mine.

His words were a promise that sparks the tension between us. The room feels too warm, my head spinning out of control. Taking a step back, I glance at his heated gaze and smile. "You're very sure of yourself, Carter."

"I am because it's true. Allow me to take you to dinner, please," he asks once more, but there's no self-assurance in his expression, merely curiosity.

"Dinner. Nothing more," I acquiesce finally.

He nods with a smile. "A friendly dinner it is."

I nod in agreement and turn to the room we're in, which is furnished with walls of bookshelves and comfortable chairs. I make my way toward the books and run my finger along the spines. "These are beautiful." They're all rare classic volumes.

"You like the classics?"

I nod, casting a quick glance at him. Turning back to the books, I follow along all the beautiful spines of gold lettering. Everything about this room is alluring, decadent, and beautiful, just like the man I can feel behind me.

His hands grip my hips and hold me still. Blood

heats as it flows through my veins, vibrating with need. "Do books turn you on, Ella? Because from where I'm standing, I think they do."

I smile at that but don't respond.

"Don't think, just feel."

I stay silent and when his hands splay on my stomach, holding my back against his chest, the heat of him searing me, I gasp.

"It sounds like the classics are your favorites."

Clearing my throat, I counter, "Are you trying to tease me, Mr. Hamilton?"

"Perhaps… it seems to be working because there's something almost sinful running through your mind right now. Isn't there?"

Even though it normally scares me being in such close proximity to a man, I don't fear him.

His lips feather against my skin and the tremble that shudders through me causes a stir in my lower stomach. My nipples are tight peaks and once again, he's turned me into someone I don't recognize.

I want him. I want to let go.

As much as I want to say no, to refuse him, I know I won't because for some unfathomable reason I know in my heart he's not the monster, he's the prince.

"Do you trust me?" His voice blankets me and calms my racing heart.

Without waiting for my answer, he turns me around, and while caging me against the bookcase, his breath fans over my face. The scent of his spicy cologne reminds me of cinnamon, and it envelops me, holding me in its warmth. And I realize it's safety.

Dragging my eyes gradually up his neck, jaw, and over those full lips, I hold my breath, and when my eyes meet his, the blue is shimmering like an ocean.

"I don't like waiting for an answer, Ms. Carmel."

My teeth bite down on my bottom lip, and his eyes darken to a stormy sea. Flicking my tongue out, I wet my lips and smile.

"I don't trust men, especially those I don't know." The words are raspy and we both hear the lust dripping from my every syllable. My pulse races. Electricity skitters over every inch of my skin and I lean back against the shelves that hold romantic words.

"What about the ones you do know?" His question is innocent enough but guts me. He's right. I shouldn't put my trust in any man. Stranger or not.

"Those are worse," I respond honestly.

"Ella, there's nothing here to fear," he promises, but I know words are just that, empty vows. I was long ago promised a stepfather who would care for me, who would love me, and nurture me. But those were all empty guarantees.

It's true, though. The men you know better than anyone, those are the monsters. They're the ones who hide in plain sight. I spent my young life hiding from the pain. The promise of a better tomorrow ensured I survived. And now I won't easily succumb to pretty words and whispered temptation.

"Carter, I said a friendly dinner. We're working together, and that's all there'll ever be." If he knew how completely shattered I truly am, there's no way he'd ever want more from me.

"We do work together," he agrees. "That means we'll be spending a lot more time together. That's where trust will grow and blossom. Let me tell you something, Ella, whatever you think you know, forget it." He leans in and my breathing accelerates, but his mouth hovers over mine, merely inches away.

I don't ever remember a feeling like the one

coursing through my veins at that moment. Emotion grips my throat violently; my lungs struggle for air. My mind flits back and forth between the here and now, and the dark memories that plague me.

He murmurs, "I don't force. I don't take what's not given. When I'm with you. When I kiss you, it will be because you asked me to. No, scrap that. It will be because you begged me to."

I want to nod, but I don't. I just watch him.

We're chest to chest and I place both palms on his sculpted shoulders. His hands trail down my arms and find my hips, gripping them, tugging me closer. Fear is at the back of my mind as I find bliss for the first time in my life and it's addictive. He's tempting me, making me want it rather than taking it without consent.

Every inch of this man has snagged me, kidnapped me, and is holding me hostage as he stares me down. He presses his body against me and I feel how much I affect him. It's only then fear crawls its way up my skin, clawing my neck and squeezing until I'm wheezing for air.

Feel that, Snowflake? That's what you do to men. You're a filthy little whore.

I push against him and he allows me space. I'm

breathing deeply, but my lungs don't want to work. Anxiety hits me. A panic attack looms around me. It's here. *He's here.* Shit.

I am strong. I am strong. I am strong.

"Ella." Concern is evident in his tone.

I take deep breaths, all the while holding on to his jacket. As if he's an anchor, a lifeline that I need to find my way to the surface while drowning in fear.

"I'm okay. It's okay."

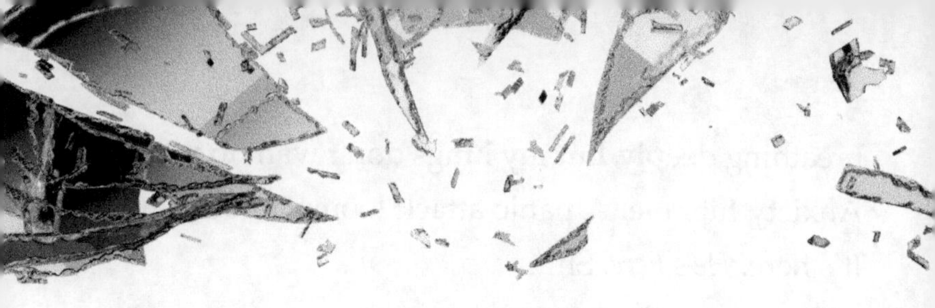

TEN

CARTER

I STEP BACK AND ALLOW HER THE FREEDOM TO CATCH her breath. Her grip on my arm tightens and I want to assure her I'm not leaving. I don't think I can. I don't think I want to.

Her perfume intoxicates me. It has me wanting to pin her against those goddamn books and fuck her until she surrenders all that's holding her hostage.

Once she's calmed, I offer her a smile and watch her relax in my hold. I need to find out what she's scared of, and once I know, I can make sure she never feels it again. This woman is going to be a temptation that will bring me to my knees.

When I look at her, I can see into her soul.

It's dark, ravaged, and pained.

I want to cure her. To see her smile. To show her pleasure.

I'm convinced she's never known pleasure. And

that in itself has me making up my mind. Bennett and I will be her medication. We'll take whatever monster lurks in the recesses of her mind and banish him for good.

I want to take her fear and give her something I haven't wanted to give anyone before. Me.

"Why me?" Her question catches me off guard. She lifts her chin and I want to smile at her indignation. She's strong. Which makes me realize it may have been the only choice she had—to pick up her pieces and keep walking. Even if she did it alone.

"You're different. I want to know you. There's something about you that intrigues me, Ella. I enjoy being tempted, enticed, and that's what you do."

She turns to me, her gaze darkening. Something haunts her at my words. I want her so much, to take her lips and swallow her moans.

"I could say the same about you, but I don't do this. I'm not the right woman for you." Her eyes drop to the floor, and she continues. "I haven't…" She turns and strokes the spines of the books again and my cock throbs to have her delicate fingers stroking me. "I mean…"

"Ella, stop, don't think." Stepping behind her

again, I cage her against the bookshelf and lower my mouth against the soft skin that taunts me. Brushing my lips lightly on the curve of her neck, I revel in the shiver of her small frame. "Just feel. Stop fighting. Drop your walls and let me in." My words whisper over the spot behind her ear and I can see another involuntary tremble she tries to hide by steeling her stance.

"Carter..." My name is a murmur on her lips that's linked directly to my throbbing erection. If I step forward, she'll feel every thick, hard inch I have for her, that I want to drive into her—deep and hard—making her chant my fucking name like a prayer. A chorus of pleasure as she comes apart beneath me.

"Ella, trust me."

Her body relaxes, and I know she's scared. Something in her eyes begs me to take it slow. If she pushes me away now, I'll find another way. Turning her to face me, I stare into her glistening eyes. They're a deep purple, capturing my attention. Her breathing is erratic. I lean in, my mouth inches from hers. Those rosy lips look good enough to eat.

Using the pad of my thumb, I swipe it slowly over her bottom lip. Perfect teeth peek at me and

I want to feel them bite into my shoulder as she unravels. "Carter, please, I—"

"Ask me. Say it." I'm now aching for her and my commanding tone sends a shiver over her. Fear lights those haunted pools and I frown. Before she can respond, a voice from behind me disturbs us, lifting the tension in the air between us.

"Mr. Hamilton, it's good to see you again."

I turn to find the owner of the hotel walking up to us.

"I didn't think you were here today, Mr. Bishop." I reach out and shake his hand.

The older man, with graying hair and dark eyes, offers me a smile. It's fake and I pick up on the anxiety in the room. His eyes flit over to Ella and she tenses beside me. She's radiating fear like it's an entity standing beside us.

"I wasn't, but I had to head back here to welcome a few guests that are checking in today. And you are?" He focuses on Ella again, and before she can respond, I do.

"This is a friend. She's joining me for dinner this evening, and I thought she'd like to see our new acquisition." He nods. "Ella, this is Mr. Bishop, the owner of this fine establishment."

Her hand that reaches to shake his trembles. Even though he doesn't notice it, I do. Snaking my arm around her waist, I feel her calm considerably, which in turn makes me smile.

"Lovely to meet you, dear. Now, Mr. Hamilton, do you have the paperwork ready?" he questions and I nod happily. This is what we came for, and I can go back to my father and give him the good news.

"All it needs is your signature."

His face drops into brief disappointment, then lifts into a smile that doesn't reach his eyes.

"Let's get to it then," he offers quietly.

We follow him out of the library, the room I'm tempted to rename a national monument after I almost took Ella against those aged bookshelves.

As I slip into the seat beside her, I watch Ella's face and all I want to do is see the smile on it again. Since we met the hotel owner she's disappeared into her shell and I want the flirty, strong woman back.

"Are you all right, Ella?"

She glances at me with a smile that doesn't

compare to the one she gave me in the library. There's pain in her gaze and I'm so fucking frustrated all I want to do is rip her fucking knickers off and fuck the darkness from her gaze.

"I am, thank you." Her words are clipped.

Needing to calm her down, I reach for her hand. As soon as my skin comes into contact with hers, heat shoots through me and the blood flowing through my veins ignites. It's as if she's my fuel and I've lit the match. I want to take her right here in the back of my car. I want to watch her body bow and hear her sweet moans. To savor those whimpers that make my dick hard.

"Do you enjoy lying to me, Ms. Carmel?"

She turns to me with a frown marring her pretty face. I can tell she's trying hide it, but I'm not blind, or stupid, and she better give me the truth now.

"I'm not lying, and I don't see how it's any of your business if I'm upset or not. We work together, Mr. Hamilton, and that's how I'd like to keep it."

I love the fire that's blazing in her eyes. I want to see them peek up at me while she's swallowing my cock. Everything is about sex. It's who I am. It's what I love. The only thing I love. And with this woman, it's no different.

She's like a siren, calling to me, and I'm about to crash into her—easily, quickly, and willingly.

Without thinking, my hand reaches up, gripping her hair by the nape of her neck, tugging her face toward mine. Our lips are mere inches apart and I can feel her warm, sweet breath on my lips. Her eyes glaze over and the tiny pinpricks of her pupils dilate into large black orbs. It's an incredible sight to see how her eye color shifts and I realize she's wearing contacts.

"Let me tell you something about me, Ella. I don't like playing games. When I ask you a fucking question, I expect an honest fucking answer, not your snotty little comments. I'll take you and show you exactly how I handle insolent women."

Her mouth drops at my retort, but the heat in her expression scorches me. I lean in and lightly feather my lips over hers. When I tighten my grip in her hair, she whimpers and my dick throbs behind my zipper. There are so many emotions running through her—fear, elation, desire, and lust—which makes me wonder what exactly she'd do if I took her to my favorite spot in the city and made her come hard.

The electric magnetism that runs between us is

alive and well.

"Carter…" She will be my fucking undoing when she whimpers my name like a needy little slut. There's nothing more I want than to be inside her right now, but I'm patient.

"Don't ever fucking lie to me again." Before she can respond, I continue, "I'm taking you to dinner this weekend."

Her brows crease and I release my hold on her hair. She didn't realize we'd pulled up to her apartment until I let her go.

"I don't think—"

"I didn't ask you to think, darling. I told you, I don't take no for an answer. Sunday. Me. You. Dinner. That gives you a day to prepare."

Baines opens her door and escorts her to the entrance of her apartment. Before he pulls away I turn to glance at her again, finding her on the threshold of her expensive home. I can't wait to tell Bennett she'll be between us soon.

Soon, darling, you'll be ours.

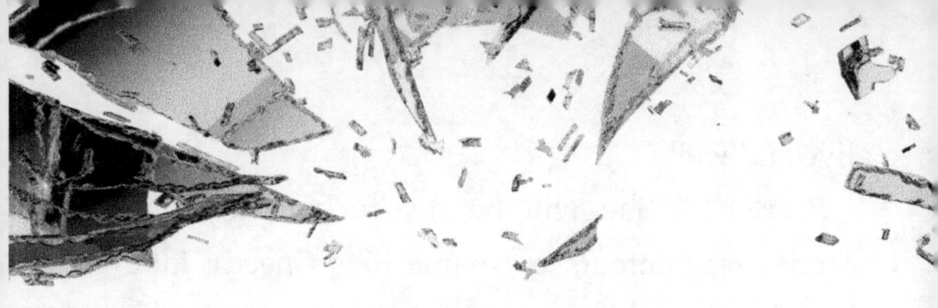

ELEVEN

ELLA

WHEN THE FRONT DOOR SHUTS, I LEAN AGAINST IT and gradually slide down until my ass hits the floor. There were so many times I should have freaked out. Too many moments when I should have turned around and run far from Carter Hamilton, but he didn't scare me.

He did something else to me. He made me ache. He pinned me with a gaze so deep, as if he could see the horrors I'd faced. His eyes pierced me, looking directly into my darkness.

Those full lips he taunted me with sent currents of desire through my body, into my veins, and as the emotion seeped into my bones I knew I was no longer the dirty little girl. I was no longer the tainted whore. I was a woman who was desired.

I toe off my heels and push up from the floor with my body still thrumming. Heading into the kitchen,

I open the fridge and grab a bottle of water, hoping it will extinguish the fire that's been lit low in my belly.

When I flop onto my sofa, I reach for the television remote and turn it on, needing something to distract me. Dinner with Carter is a bad idea. In fact, it's a terrible idea. But I know I'm not going to be able to stay away from him.

The images on screen do nothing to drag my attention away from Mr. Hamilton and I know I have no choice but to let this play out. As long as he doesn't find out about my past. *Would it be so bad to go for dinner?* It's just one date. Even as the thought comes to me, I know it's a lie. He doesn't look like a man who'd just walk away from something he wants. And for some reason, he wants me.

Rolling over in bed, I groan, knowing I have to go into the office, even though it's a Saturday. I reach for my phone and find a message from Carter.

Carter: *Good morning, Princess. I trust you'll have a good day. I will because you're on my mind.*

This message is evidence enough that he doesn't take no for an answer. I'm not used to it. All my past relationships, if you can call them that, I've pushed the men away when they got too pushy or forceful and none of them pursued me after that. They'd all walked away happily from me. But Carter, he's different. He's definitely forceful, but even so, the fear that normally cripples me doesn't come.

Me: *Do you always message women who don't agree to go out with you?*

Carter: *Especially those. Did I mention I love a challenge?*

With his snarky reply, I can't stop the giggle that escapes my lips. As if I'm a teenager with her first boyfriend. In so many respects, I suppose I am. I've never really been through this flirty stage with someone. The few I have been with were merely innocent blind dates, nothing more.

There weren't flowers and messages. And then there was the monster who took and took even though I didn't give. Before I can respond, my phone buzzes. Sliding my finger across the screen, I answer the man who's made a charm of hummingbirds' flutter about in my belly.

"Hello," I answer, my voice still raspy from sleep.

"Ella," he whispers the word as if he's caressing it. "I wanted to hear your voice."

I smile. My face aches with all the grinning he's made me do. He breathes steadily into the phone, which seems to calm me.

"And this is my voice. How are you today?" I question, finding myself flirting easily.

"I'm tempted to pick you up and take you to work. Do you think you'd want to spend time alone in the car with me?" he quips and I can hear the smirk on his face.

"Perhaps. No funny business?" I question in jest, trying to lighten my tone, but fail when I hear his heavy sigh. It's clear he's trying and I'm still so fucking scared.

"Ella, I may be a pain in the arse, but I'll never make you do something you don't want to. Come on, I'm heading in to see Bennett anyway," he responds.

"Fine, you can pick me up. I'll be ready in an hour."

"Perfect, I'll see you soon, Princess."

With that he hangs up and I close my eyes, savoring the word princess as I replay it in my head, recalling his gravelly timbre. Pushing off the bed, I head into the bathroom and start getting ready. If he's that adamant to woo me, I'll give him a chance.

Exactly an hour after his call the buzzer for my apartment rings through the expansive kitchen and living room. Dropping the yogurt container in the trash, I head to answer before it rings again. "Hello, Carter."

"Ella, would you like me to come up?" His tone is light and I can tell he's smiling.

"It's okay, I'll be down in a few minutes." Before he can respond, I hang up and grab my purse. I've decided on a black knee-length woolen dress that's warm enough I don't need a coat. In the elevator, I inhale deep, calming breaths, hoping to relax before I come face-to-face with the man who haunted my dreams.

As the silver doors slide open, he steps forward and immediately my heart leaps into my throat, thrumming wildly at how sexy he is. Those eyes that shimmer like the ocean at night with the reflection of the moon in them. There's a dark dusting of stubble on his angular jaw and his tousled hair looks as if he's run his hand through it a few times.

Dressed in an exquisite charcoal Armani suit and a crisp white dress shirt, he looks like he should be on the cover for the most eligible bachelor. And he probably is.

"Ella." He holds out a hand while rolling my name off his tongue as if its taste is the only thing he needs to survive. There's a husky tone to his voice, reminding me of a smoky scotch.

"Carter." Lifting my mouth into a shy smile, I slip my hand in his and we make our way out to the car.

"You look lovely. Are you sure you're not going to be cold?" He assesses me with a gaze that screams desire, but I don't recoil. Instead, I shiver with anticipation.

"I'll survive," I quip as his driver opens the door, allowing me into the sleek, black SUV. Once I'm seated comfortably, he joins me shifting close enough to have our thighs touching. The heat of his body warms me instantly. "Thank you for picking me up. I could have taken a cab." I sneak a glance at him, taking in his masculine profile.

"I wanted to see you again. What better way to spend the morning on my way to work than with a beautiful woman?" he says with a poised elegance. He's quiet for a moment as if choosing his words carefully, then continues, "Also, I figured it's a good way to get to know you." The side of his mouth lifts playfully and he turns his gaze on me.

"What do you want to know?"

"What's your favorite food?" The question isn't what I'm expecting, but he looks like he truly wants to know.

"Sushi." My answer earns me a handsome grin.

"Interesting," is all he murmurs before turning to the window, but my shallow breaths can be heard in the silence. How can two words disarm me so much? "Do you enjoy the outdoors, or do you prefer staying in?"

I consider his question for a moment before answering. "Both. It depends on my mood. There are times I love being outdoors, and sometimes, it's nice to relax on the sofa, with a good book and a glass of wine."

"Mmm," he hums, the sound smooth and decadent, as if he's trying to blanket me in it. "What about your favorite movie?" He smirks the question, sending a flurry of butterflies to my belly.

Once again, the question isn't something I'd

think he'd ask, which makes me smile. "There are so many amazing movies. I don't think I could choose just one." I glance at him, and it's true. I've never had a favorite movie, but there are some that tug at my heart that I could watch over and over again.

"And your favorite fairy tale? Don't tell me it's Cinderella." This time he laughs, a full throaty one and I can't stop my own giggle. He's infectious in a way I was missing for so long.

"I suppose that would be one that could tell my story, although I never had a stepmother who was evil." I shrug, realizing I'm once again giving away more than I should.

"So, you have a tendency of running away from handsome men, Princess?" he murmurs.

"Who said you were handsome?" This time I tease him, earning myself a smile that lights up his face. The attraction between us is evident.

"Well"—he shifts on the bench seat to face me—"you seem to be affected by me," he whispers knowingly, his knuckles feathering over my cheek, "and I'm certainly affected by you." He leans in and his lips brush the sensitive spot behind my ear, causing a shudder to wrack through me. My heart catapults itself into my throat, choking me with emotion.

He sits back and I miss his warmth. Before he has time to ask another question or I have time to respond, the car pulls up to the offices of Ainsworth International. Carter opens his door and exits the vehicle. Turning, he offers me his hand, which I accept. As soon as mine slips into his, electricity jolts through me, setting my body alight with want.

Once I'm beside him on the sidewalk, he releases me and I immediately miss his touch. What's wrong with me? We walk, side by side, toward the entrance. Entering together, I find Lizzie's glance trained on us. "Mr. Hamilton, good morning." She offers a shy smile, then turns her attention on me. "Ella, you've got a meeting with a new client today. Mr. Hernandez. It's in your diary."

I nod graciously as we pass. "Thank you, Lizzie." I know she'll be asking why I've arrived with him this morning and I think my boss will be wondering the same thing. At the elevator, Carter pushes the button, waiting beside me as the numbers light up. The air is alive, swirling, heavy with want.

Silver doors slide open, allowing us to enter the empty car.

"I'm glad you agreed to my offer, Ella. I'd like

to see more of you. Besides our dinner, of course. Perhaps I can give you a ride every morning to work?" Carter doesn't look at me. He talks to the doors, but it feels as if his heated gaze is on me.

Darting my eyes to him, I take in the profile of the man beside me.

Poised, elegant, handsome. Unbelievably so.

His tanned skin seems darker with the dusting of stubble on his jaw. His black hair, dark as night, has me itching to tangle my finger through the thick, silky strands.

"I think I'd like that." My response is nothing more than a whisper, but he hears. And just like that, I've given him a sliver of trust. More than I've given any man, ever.

Once we reach the top floor, the elevator spits us out and I head directly to my desk, while Carter follows behind me. He leans in as I drop my bag, his cologne once again engulfing me in its safety.

"I'll collect you when you're finished with work this afternoon. Till later, Ella."

And with that he turns on his heel and strolls confidently to Bennett's office and disappears behind the thick wooden door, shutting it with a resounding click.

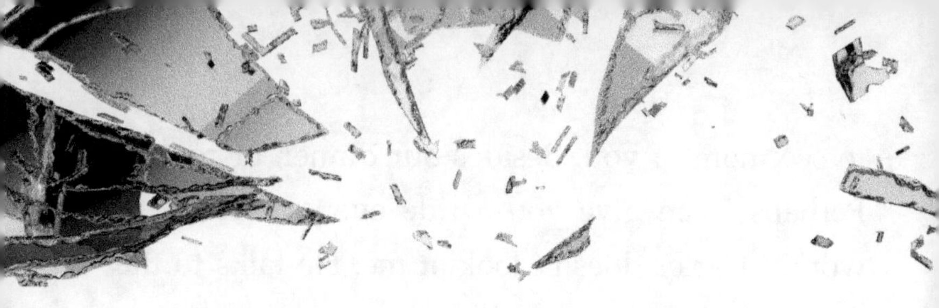

TWELVE

BENNETT

THE DOOR SHUTS AND I DRAG MY ATTENTION AWAY from the email up to my best friend. His smirk is enough to tell me something happened. And if something happened, I know I'm in for the whole sordid story.

Details, he loves details.

"And? You're not going to tell me you've already gotten into those knickers of hers, are you?"

He unties the button on his suit jacket and settles in the champagne-colored suede chair opposite my desk. He rests one ankle over the opposite knee, looking ever the playboy he's known to be.

"I didn't fuck her, but"—he pauses for dramatic effect—"I'm taking her for dinner tomorrow night," he confesses with pride, confidence shining in his smirk. "We'll soon have her tangled in our web. I assure you. However, I did learn that our girl is

114

utterly broken. She's fearful of something."

"What do you think it is?" Concern drips from my every word.

He glances at the window, concentrating on the city. His eyes give it away. He likes her. I haven't seen him care for someone before. Not like this.

"I'm not sure. She doesn't like talking about her family. I have a feeling that might be the reason," he tells me earnestly.

My heart constricts. I haven't spent enough time with her, but if he's this worried about her, then I am too.

"I'll talk to her today. We are meeting with a client then I'll take her to lunch. What are you doing here anyway?"

He shrugs and pushes off the chair, rising to full height. "I needed an excuse to be alone with her after yesterday, so I told her I was coming to see you." His confession has me shaking my head.

"Starting off with lies isn't a good idea. Perhaps you should be honest with her. There's no need for you to be fucking with her head, especially if she's so broken." I admonish him as if he were a child, but I hate when he plays his games with women.

"It's not her head I'm interested in right now."

He regards me and I wait for him to tell me he's about to fuck her and chuck her when he continues, "I want her secrets."

"What?" Surprise is evident in my tone.

Without meeting my eyes, he's still focused on the window that overlooks the city below. "I want to see what she holds in her heart, Bennett."

"You think she'll want that? To date you, or us?" My question is incredulous and the shock on my face must be evident.

"Yes." He sounds confident that this woman who's seemingly fragile is going to want to date two men. "She's hiding something and I intend to find out what it is. Her trust is non-existent, so I need your help." He glances at me then.

"You're the one who handles the first two steps," I tell him, but I know what he wants. We've done this before. Broken a girl down together and helped her heal.

His blue eyes pin me, meeting my green ones with earnest. "She'll submit to us, allow us in. If she can trust both of us, there's no telling what we can do. We both need this, Bennett. You know that as much as I do. This time, we need to play it differently."

It takes a lot for Carter Hamilton to change the

rules like this. It's not in his nature to confess he's not capable of doing something on his own. He's every bit a dominant even when he can't admit it. Or doesn't want to admit it.

Ella is incredibly beautiful. I know I can easily sway her. She just needs to learn what we are to each other. But, since my best friend needs me, I'm game.

"Fine, I'll do it."

When Carter left, I didn't see Ella at her desk and I knew she was in the meeting with Alejandro Hernandez. One of London's poster boys, perfect, straight-laced, and the name on all women's lips. I've known him for about six months, or should I say, known of him. He's been topping the most eligible bachelor list alongside my best friend for a couple of months now.

"Bennett." Ella's sultry voice comes from the doorway.

When I lift my gaze to skim over her body, I find myself hardening for a taste. Carter's right, I do want her, and I've seen her body respond to me. Her eyes are like windows into her mind and right now, it's as if the sun is shining through them.

Dressed in office attire this woman could walk a fucking runway, and I imagine her in nothing but some lace knickers and a bra to match and my desire skyrockets.

"How did the meeting with Mr. Hernandez go?" I question. Crooking my fingers, I call her to me. She's submissive. Her body reeks of it, because at my order, her eyelids flutter and she obeys. Easily, without question, she just does it.

Carter must have noticed. That's why he's so adamant to own her. To claim her.

She sighs. "It went well, but…"

I watch as she settles herself in the seat Carter was in earlier.

"He's being stubborn about signing the purchase agreement. He wants another week to think it over. I did, however, manage to talk him into doing it in three days, but that's as far as he'd budge." She's incredible.

"I'm impressed, Ms. Carmel. That's something I haven't been able to do with that man. Tell me"—I lean forward, holding her hostage with one look—"what did you agree to do for him that got him to drop his week to three days?"

"He asked me to put in a good word with Lizzie." She shrugs then drops her gaze to the floor.

So damn submissive, it's beautiful.

"And does my receptionist know this?" Tipping my head to the side, I watch her cheeks flush and she nods. I realize she has a nervous tick when she runs her finger over her lips. At the moment, she's got her thumb swiping back and forth on her plump lower lip and it's hypnotic.

"I've spoken to her, she does like him, but she's shy to talk to him." She shrugs, sitting back.

I watch her blouse strain against her breasts and I'm dying to feel how those amazing tits fit in my hands.

"Okay, I've got a proposal for you." Lifting my mouth into a smirk, I watch her dark brows lift in question. "There's a charity event tomorrow night. I'd like to take you. Not a date. It's purely professional. There are people I need to introduce you to, and Carter will be there, so you'll be able to spend time with him, see him in his element."

She tips her head to the side and watches me, narrowing her gaze. This is what Hamilton and I agreed to. It's her first test and I wonder if she'll pass.

Shaking her head in confusion, she responds, "But I've been invited to dinner with Carter tomorrow night." Her fingers lace through each other. There's a slight tremble that travels through her.

Rising, I stalk to the other side of my desk. As soon as I near her, the soft scent of orange blossoms assaults my nose. Delicious and sweet.

"Yes, that will be after the dinner. You'll join him before the event, and me at the event." It already sounds like the perfect plan to get her into our bed.

"Okay, is this going to be formal?" she questions with a small smile and I nod.

"Yes, it's black tie. Since it's a business event I'm inviting you to, I'll be paying for everything. Since this is quite sudden, with it being tomorrow night, I want you to leave early, take the company credit card, and purchase an outfit, dress, shoes, whatever accessories you'll need."

I wanted to take her for lunch, but this is even better. We'll both play with her tomorrow night until she's begging for more. I pull my wallet from my pocket and pull out the black credit card. No limit. Her eyes pop open wide as she regards the plastic.

"Thank you, Bennett. I appreciate that."

When I hand her the card my fingertips brush against her fingers and a small shiver runs through her. It's slight, but I see it. I've been with too many women not to know all those little tells. And this right here is Ella's when she's turned on. I know that because her pupils have dilated and her cheeks are flushed.

"I'll see you later, Ella. I have a meeting downtown and I'll head straight home after." She nods and rises, holding on to the card.

"Take care, and"—she glances at me over her shoulder with those alluring pools—"thank you." With that, she walks out with her hips swaying hypnotically and I'm hard for her.

I need to fuck her.

I'm hungry and she'll satiate that pang soon enough.

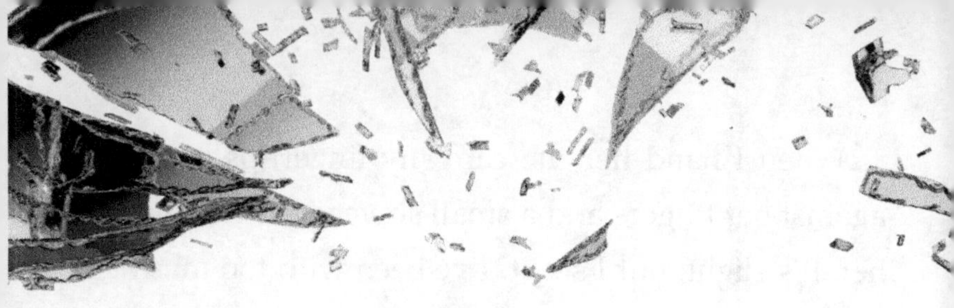

THIRTEEN

ELLA

MY DINNER WITH CARTER, FOLLOWED BY THE charity function with Bennett is tonight. To say I'm nervous would be an understatement. The floor-length dress I bought is black lace, with a silk lining that covers my intimate areas. It's got a low cut back. It's elegant, understated, and sleek. Hugging my curves, but not showing too much skin.

I hold it up against my chin and glance at my appearance in the mirror. I haven't worn something so risqué before because I've always felt self-conscious when people—men—look at me, but with Carter and Bennett it's different. With them I feel safe.

Pulling my underwear drawer open, I grab a matching set of charcoal lingerie. A night of silk and lace seems to be the order of the day. It's dark in the room with the moon being hidden behind some clouds. My heart leaps into my throat.

Fear grips me so suddenly, I lose my breath. A smell wafts into the apartment from the open terrace door, a familiar scent. My mind races with images I'd buried. My body shudders with revulsion and I'm transported to that fearful sixteen-year-old girl once again.

I'm strong. I'm strong. I'm strong.

The mantra doesn't help because as I step into the main area of the bedroom, I find the terrace doors still open. My gaze settles on my bed. The sight assaults me, sending me into a black hole. In the dark, the vile monster is there, clawing his way toward me. *It's in my head. It's not real.* But it continues to drag me, like a hand gripping my ankle and pulling me along with the evil, the dark, and the sinister.

Dropping to my knees, I stare at the object. A nondescript shiny, sparkly object that looks just like I remember it. The only problem is… *I don't want to remember it.*

"Do you like your present, Snowflake?" His cold gray eyes stare at me.

My mother is in the living room. If I scream she'll hear me, but I know she won't believe me. I've become a prisoner in my bedroom and all I want to do is escape. He leans in. Stale breath from his lunch fans over my face and my body convulses as I wretch.

"Fucking answer me, little whore." Spittle sprays over my face as he hisses.

"Yes, yes, I do." My hands are shaking and I'm scared that I'm about to drop the fucking thing. It's shiny, and when you shake it the white particles are meant to imitate snow. Small buildings within the globe, one I recognize as Buckingham Palace, and there's a tiny red bus inside as well. I wonder if I could ever run away to another country where he couldn't find me.

Before he can continue, my mother walks into my room, oblivious to the scene before her. It's as if she's drugged and can't face reality. "I'm heading to bed, you two." She leans in and kisses me on the forehead before giving her husband a kiss on the lips. His hands reach down and squeezes her against him, but when I glance up, his eyes are pinned on me.

"Good night, Snowflake." They turn and leave me in my room.

Placing the globe on my nightstand, I get under the covers and face the window so I can drown in the dark outside. As I stare at the moon, I promise myself one day I'm going to fly away, to London, where he can't find me. But will I ever be safe from him?

My eyes snap open and I feel him behind me. I must have fallen asleep. My hands are bound to the bed and I can't see in the dark. It's only when I move my head that I realize there's something covering my eyes. He's blindfolded me.

I'm strong, I'm strong. I'm strong.

"Look at my pretty Snowflake."

I can feel the cold air on my skin which causes me to shiver. Rough, calloused hands grope me, pressing into my soft flesh. Tears burn behind the material and I whimper, begging through the material he's stuffed in my mouth. I know what it is, but I don't want the reality to set in just yet.

Suddenly, the blindfold is ripped away and I watch him use it to tie one ankle to the foot end of my bed. He uses a scarf to tie the other ankle and I'm now naked and spread open to his disgusting glare.

"Do you like your panties in your mouth, my sweet girl?"

My head lolls from side to side and I know he can see the fear in my eyes. It feeds his vile need. He reaches for something on my nightstand and when he kneels between my legs, I gasp into the material gagging me. His fingers plunge into my core, opening me painfully and I scream into the makeshift gag.

The pain is coming. The pain is coming. The pain is coming.

Without warning, his fingers are replaced by the round glass orb and I cry out, but my sounds are muffled. Pushing the snow globe into me, he twists it around. The sinister smile on his face has my body retching and my throat burns with bile that sits in my esophagus and I can't swallow.

"Look how pretty you are, spread open wide. You like that, don't you? Can you see what you do to me?" His hand wraps around his shaft, stroking it. Tears stream down the side of my face and onto the pillow below me.

He pulls out the object and pushes it back in, fucking me with the present he bought. As he forces it into me I fear it may shatter while inside my body. His hand moves faster, both ramming the object into me and getting himself off.

He stops and his body locks, as he shoots thick white streams of cum all over my mound and stomach. When he finally relieves me of the object, I close my eyes, thankful that it's over. "Open your fucking eyes."

I obey. It's the only thing I can do. I don't have a choice.

I never have a choice.

"Watch me enjoy your sweetness."

I'm forced to watch him lick the glass, tasting me, savoring what he's just done.

"Broken little Snowflake. No man will want you. You're filthy. A disgusting, tainted whore."

Fear takes hold of my heart, and revulsion has me dry heaving as my body wracks with sobs. My stomach tightens with anxiety as my heart thuds in my ears like a drum. A warning.

"No, no, no... please," I beg to nobody in particular. I don't pray, because no God will save me from this nightmare. On my bed is the very object from the nightmare that's haunted me most of my life.

My throat tightens, like it did every night for two years of hearing my bedroom door being pushed open and heavy footfalls making their way toward me. When my body was taken and used, I became nothing more than a fuck toy for my stepfather to enjoy.

He was right. I can never move on.

I'll never be able to be a normal girl.

No man on this earth would want someone like

me.

I want to curl into a ball on the plush carpet and cry, but I've been strong for too long. So, I steel myself, take a deep breath, and push this emotion, this fear and anger into the back of my mind, into the box where I've kept the years of agony.

Rushing to the patio door, I shut it with a loud bang, locking it with trembling fingers. I don't look at the bed. I can't. The offending item sits there, taunting me.

I'll always find you.

I race to the bathroom, opening the bottle of tablets I've been taking for the past four years. Swallowing two down, I close my eyes and breathe through the fear. I can't let him win. It must be a hallucination. I'm so broken I see things. The doctors said it was part of the trauma I suffered.

I'd see the monster in the dark. I'd hear his voice.

I thought I was going mad. Until the pills helped me silence him. With traveling and work, I forgot to take them for two days, and this is the price I pay. When I finally open my eyes, I watch the mascara streaking down my face.

Focusing on tonight, I wash up, but when I reach my bedroom once more, it's gone. It wasn't real. I breathe a sigh of relief. It's not really there. Swallowing the lump in my throat, I get ready for the event and dinner.

FOURTEEN

CARTER

"*D*O YOU UNDERSTAND WHAT A FUCK-UP THIS IS?" MY *father's dark eyes smolder with anger. They're red hot and they're directed at me.*

I nod. There's nothing else I can do because I know I'm in deep shit.

"Yes. I know. But—"

"No, Carter, no fucking buts. You've done this for the very last time. I can't bail you out every time you decide to act like a fucking arsehole. You're old enough to know how to act responsibly, or do I need to teach you that too?"

"No, Father." It's not the first time I'm being reprimanded by him and I doubt it will be the last. He's trying to be proud of me and all I feel is disdain. For him. For my life. I just want to be a normal nineteen-year-old. Is that too much to ask?

"This will all be yours, son. When you turn twenty-

one you'll become my second-in-command. Remember that as a Hamilton, you need to keep up appearances. So, we need to write a check, which you will deliver. Is that understood?" The man I've grown up to call father is telling me my future, and all I want to do is run from it. It's been like this since I can remember—the grooming and planning. Me and my sister have had our lives set out for us since we were born.

"Yes, Father." This is one of my biggest fuck-ups. I can tell he's holding back and he's right. I almost fucked up my entire life because of one stupid night.

"Carter, if I have to keep cleaning up your mess I don't see a future for you. I'm your father, but you need to learn responsibility." His glare is evident and I know I should have been more responsible. My father has paid my way for years. Every time I messed up and made mistakes he was there.

Call it teen angst, but after being told what to do all your life, there are times you want to break out of the mold. "Father, I'm nineteen, I'm bound to make mistakes." Pushing up from the chair, I stalk to the office door. He practically lives here, and I know it's because of the pretty woman outside.

Maybe that's where I get it from. My playboy ways. My father loves women, it's no secret, and he's been *fucking the woman he calls his assistant for years.*

"This is no fucking joke, Carter. Here, take this and sort your shit out. I'm not going to say it again and I'm not going to do this again. If you're going to act like a spoilt brat, you'll be brought down so fast your head will spin." He hands me the piece of paper that's meant to fix everything. One million pounds.

That's nothing to him, a small sum of money to make sure his son looks like a saint. Well, I'm no saint, and he better remember that. I realize then and there that I do not want to be like him.

"Thank you." There's nothing more to say as I walk out of his office with a piece of paper that will save my future.

Shaking my head of the memory, I pull on my black tuxedo jacket. I take one last look in the mirror and wonder if Ella will be able to handle me. *Will she obey me? Let me take what I want?*

Picking up my phone, I open my messages and send her one.

Me: *Ella, I'm almost ready. Send me a photo of your dress, so I can match my tie to it.*

As soon as I hit send, I can't help the smirk that plays on my lips. I know she'll obey. It's in her nature. I don't wait long and my phone beeps. Sliding my thumb over the screen, the message pops up with a photo of the dress she bought with a short message.

Ella: *I think you'll find it easy to match black with black, Carter.*

She's fucking beautiful and the thought of her in black lace hugging her curves has me hard as rock. Her body is perfect for anything she chooses to wear, but there's something about lace that tempts me. *Who am I kidding?* She's my temptation, slowly becoming my obsession.

I know Bennett has invited her to the charity event, which only works in our favor. We'll easily get her to submit to us. The thought of finally finding a woman we can claim as our own excites me. Never before has someone intrigued me the way Ella has.

What I wouldn't do to climb inside her mind and learn every thought she has. To know what she's hiding behind those beautiful eyes, to have those perfect lips spill the dirty secrets that hold her hostage. My body craves her and I've only known her for a few days.

I head into my living room and the intercom chimes. *Shit.* As I open the door my sister bounds in.

"Carter, I'm so excited. I spoke to Father and he said I—" She stops when she turns to take in my appearance. "You're looking particularly poised and sharp." Her frown is adorable. My sister is twenty-nine, but there are times I'm certain she's still a teenager.

"I'm trying to impress. Now what are you doing here? Shouldn't you be getting ready?" I head into the kitchen. Her footfalls behind me clink on the tiles.

"Who is she, Carter?"

Ignoring her question, I open the fridge and hand her a beer. My sister acts like the perfect elegant woman in front of my parents, but I know deep down that's not who she is. She accepts the bottle with a smile while staring at me, waiting for my response.

"What do you mean?"

"Don't fucking lie to me. I can see this is for a woman. Is she beautiful?" My sister is insistent; she always has been. Curious like a little kid wanting to know everything. Even when she knows some things will hurt her. Like when she found out about my father having an affair with his secretary.

"Fine. She's my new real estate broker. I'm taking her for dinner and she'll be joining Bennett at the event tonight. I don't need you to approve. She's lovely and this is purely a business dinner."

"Oh please, brother, you'd never take a woman to a business dinner. I'm sure by the end of the night you'll be knuckle deep inside her." There's one thing about my sister. She's brutally honest. She calls it like she sees it and I love her for it, but my sex life isn't one of the things I want her analyzing.

"Kat, finish your beer and show yourself out. I'll see you later." I lean in and plant a soft kiss on her forehead then head to the door.

"Enjoy your latest obsession, brother."

Her giggle is the last thing I hear before shutting my front door.

My sister is right. Ella has become something of an obsession over the past few days, and I won't stop until she's divulged what's hurting her. I want everything. Her secrets, her body, and her mind. And if I get her heart in the process, then I'll take that too. Don't get me wrong, love is something I crave, but my life hasn't afforded me the luxury. I've coveted too many things that weren't mine.

Don't judge me before you know my background. Women beg and plead with me to take them, to fuck them mercilessly, because their husbands aren't around to do it. And what normal red-blooded male would say no to a woman on her knees?

I love watching women come, to see their eyes glisten with desire and feel their bodies pulse with release. To taste that sweetness is like a drug to me. It's an addiction.

Fifteen minutes later Baines pulls up to the pavement outside Ella's building, and I get out of the car. Walking up to the entrance, I push the glass door open and smile at the doorman. "I'm here to see Ms. Carmel. What's her apartment number?" He offers me a smile, but I can tell he's wary.

I told Bennett I'd be picking her up and he agreed. We're playing this like we would any other woman. With us, there's no escape.

"I'll buzz her." He picks up the white phone and pushes four buttons. *Six. Nine. Six. Nine.*

Turning my attention to the foyer, I take in the artwork on the walls and scan the old paintings of London back in the heyday as they like to call it.

The lift pinging has me turning around and the sight I'm met with astounds me. Ella in a black lace figure-hugging dress looks like an angel walking out of the fires of hell and all I want to do is take her back into the sinful darkness with me.

Her long hair is in loose waves down her back and she has smoky eye makeup on, which only accentuates her amethyst eyes. "Carter." Her voice is ragged, which has me tipping my head to the side. And when she nears I can see her cheeks are flushed. She's been crying.

"Are you all right?" I step toward her and reach out, but as soon as my hand touches hers, I notice her flinch. I wait impatiently for her response, needing an answer. I would never hurt her.

Why would she be afraid of me?

"I'm fine. Can we go?"

My gaze is trained on her. She's shorter than me and as I peer down at her she lifts her chin. She's trying to be strong when all she wants to do is break down. *A fragile princess.* I nod, lacing my fingers through hers, guiding her to the waiting car.

Once we're seated and Baines pulls away I take in her stoic expression. The carefree girl from yesterday is gone and I need to know what happened. "Are you going to tell me? Or do I have to torture you to get an answer?" I chuckle, but stop when she glares at me. *That's new.*

"I don't enjoy being forced to do something I don't want to." Her tone is clipped, but when I reach for her, she allows me to slip my hand in hers.

"Trust me, Princess. If I want you to do something"—I lean in, allowing the next words to whisper over her—"it will be for your pleasure."

"And what if I don't find pleasure? What if I'm not made that way?"

Her words stop me cold. I can't help staring at her. Long moments pass, but her question hangs in the air between us. I'm about to answer when the car stops and Baines announces we've arrived at our destination.

Opening my door, I slip out and offer my hand to her, not expecting her to take it, but she does and I can't help the satisfaction that blossoms inside me. Once she steps from the car, her lips part on a gentle gasp. It's an exquisite sound, one I'd like to hear more often.

"This is incredible." She takes in the glass building.

The Shard, one of London's newer developments,

and I've booked out a private dining room for us at the Aqua Shard, with a view of the city below, while we're dining.

I haven't forgotten what she said earlier, and there's no way she hasn't experienced pleasure before. *What the fuck does that even mean?*

Once we're seated, I glance at her. The awe in her beautiful features is breathtaking and I find myself staring at her. She turns to face me again and a smile plays on her lips.

"This is much more than I expected, Carter. You didn't have to—"

"I did. I wanted to."

The waiting staff appear with the wine I pre-ordered and proceed to fill her glass and mine.

"Do you trust me?" It's the same question I asked her previously when she informed me trust was difficult for her.

She gazes at me for a moment, then shrugs. "I'll try."

"It's all I ask." Looking up at the young waitress, I see the blush on her cheeks when I offer her a smile. "Can we have two of your chef's special, the salmon fillet?"

She nods and spins on her heel, leaving me alone

with Ella.

"Do you bring all your women here?" Her question has me chuckling. She sounds jealous.

"All my women? Does my reputation precede me that much?" Lifting the wine glass, I take a sip while watching her reaction.

Her gaze drops to my mouth and I can't help teasing her by licking my lips.

"Yes, I suppose being a rich man like yourself, you must have many women falling over themselves for your attention." She's right, but right now there's only one woman who has it.

"I do, but you're the one with me right now and I'm curious if you're willing to experience what I have to offer." The energy that surrounds us is at a boiling point as desire swirls around her. I'm tempted to touch her, to make her whimper. I love playing in public. The taboo of getting caught heightens the senses.

She lifts her glass and takes another sip. Her lips shimmer with the liquid and I can't help myself from leaning in and as our eyes meet, I can see the fear evident in her gaze.

"Trust me." My words are a soft murmur and she doesn't flinch. Lifting my hand, I tip her chin so I have better access to those plump lips. "May I?"

She nods. It's quick and unsure, but I have to do this.

My lips brush over hers. Her breathing turns ragged. Her pupils dilate. They're the color of the sky as the sun sets and night falls. My tongue darts out and slowly traces the curve of her lips, tasting the wine from them. My dick is so hard while images of drizzling wine over her body and licking it off have me groaning, but this time I don't hide it. "You're beautiful, Ella. I want to taste you."

Her gasp is loud, and all I can do is smile.

"Carter, I think—"

"Stop thinking, just feel. Let go and experience it. Let the pleasure take over all your senses and allow me to show you what it feels like. You're fragile. Aren't you?" My words cause her to whimper. Unshed tears shine in her amethyst gaze.

"Only in the dark," she confesses. It's the first real statement she's made while looking directly at me. Raw and honest.

My other hand lifts to her arm and I trail a featherlight touch down her bare arm. When goosebumps rise on her skin I can't help smiling. I know she wants me because it's written all over her face. "Do you want to take the lead?" I question softly.

"I don't know how to do this."

We stare at each other for a few moments and I take in the innocence that's so clear in her features.

"Do what feels natural. But let me warn you, this is the one and only time I'll allow you to be in control. Normally, I'll be in charge, and you'll love every fucking moment," I warn her with a feral grunt.

She lifts her chin and I love the cheekiness I see on her face. "Then do it."

The fear I saw earlier is gone and I realize this is my moment. She's allowing me in. A sneak peek behind her high walls and I'd be stupid if I didn't take it. I take a gulp of wine and turn to her. Gripping her hair at the nape of her neck, I pull her body against mine, then without warning my mouth crashes down on hers and we share the chilled Chardonnay while our tongues fight in a sexually charged dance that has me wanting to have our bodies connected in more places than just our mouths.

Her body becomes pliable, molding to mine, and I swallow the whimpers from her, reveling in her taste. She's more potent than any drug. She's more intoxicating than any alcohol, and I'm addicted.

Our moment is broken when the waitress brings our food. Placing each of the plates on the table, she moves away and the hostess enters the private dining area.

"Mr. Hamilton, I apologize for the intrusion, but I have something for your guest." She hands Ella a small silver envelope and box.

Once we're alone, I'm intrigued as I watch a myriad of emotions flit over my girl's face.

I watch Ella open it and pull out a single card, also silver, with a large white snowflake on the front. Her worried gaze darts to me, and there's emotion stronger than fear running through them. There's revulsion, horror, and panic.

"Is this your idea of a joke?" She tears the card, but all I can do is frown.

"I have no idea what you're talking about, Ella. I didn't send it."

We stare at each other and I hope she can see the truth in my eyes, because I have no idea what that meant to her, but whatever it is, she's got pure agony on her face. She rips the box open and inside there's a small winter snow globe. I remember Kat used to have them as a girl. They were her favorite ornaments.

"It's… The card… You didn't…"

"No, I didn't. What's got you so worked up, baby?"

Shaking her head, she pushes up from the table and rushes toward the restroom. My body is vibrating with fear and confusion. Without thinking I follow her. As soon as I push the door open I find her huddled over in a corner. Her face is streaked with tears.

She's fragile. Delicate. Broken. A flower about to lose its petals.

"Go away, please. Just leave me," she begs me, but I can't bring myself to walk out. Kneeling before her, I place a hand on her knee.

"I'm not going anywhere. I'm right here for you. Talk to me, Ella." Her tears flow freely and the well put together woman falling apart in front of me is a scared little girl and the only thing I want to do is hold her. "Can I touch you?"

She nods and I scoot closer, pulling her into my arms. I cocoon her body with mine.

"He's here. I need to go home. He's here." Her words are ragged, as if she's swallowed a cupful of sand and what it does to my heart is concerning.

It's never been an issue. I've kept it far away from affection, but with her, Ella Carmel, I want to give it all to her. She's going to be my downfall, and I'd gladly take the leap.

"Who, baby? Who's here?" Her gaze meets mine, glistening with emotion. Tears stream down her cheeks and she shakes her head.

"Him. He's found me."

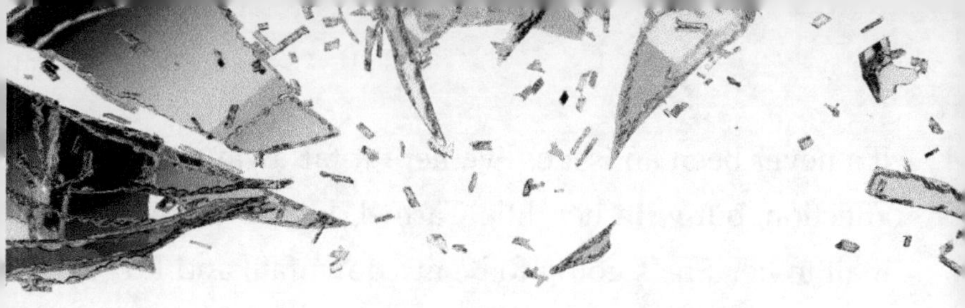

FIFTEEN

ELLA

CARTER STARES AT ME FOR SO LONG I THINK HE hasn't heard me, but then he nods. Pulling me up, he wraps his arms around me and practically carries me out of the restroom. "Where are… where are we going?" My voice is croaky at best and he halts, staring at me.

"I'm taking you home and you're going to tell me exactly what the hell is going on. No more secrets. No more lies." His voice is adamant as we pass the hostess where he offers her a curt nod and we hasten our way down to the waiting car.

Cold settles heavily in my bones. "Carter, please," I beg, but I don't know what I'm asking for. He startles me when his eyes meet mine. There's fear and concern floating in them.

"I'm taking you home. I need to make a quick appearance at my father's event, but Bennett will stay with you while I'm gone. You're not to be alone. Okay?"

I can't argue with that. As Baines drives through London streets taking me home, I can't help the sinking feeling that my past is catching up to me.

I've let down my guard. I've allowed a man inside my mind, and if I'm honest I like it. Carter gives me a sense of safety in his dominance, but also it's as if he heals me. Like he's taking every broken piece of the girl I once was and molding her into a woman. Where desire and need isn't something to be feared but embraced.

"Come," he murmurs and I realize I've lost time because we're outside my apartment building. He helps me out of the car, my knees still wobbly from the shock and fear that wracked my body. When Carter's gaze lands on mine, it's as if he's looking into my soul, finding all the ugly parts, dragging them to the surface, only to cleanse me. "You're safe, baby. I swear to you," he promises, scooping me up and carrying me bridal style into the lobby.

At the elevators, he leans in and I push the button.

Everything is done in silence. Wordless understanding.

There's no need to vocalize anything because

this man knows me. It should scare me, but I feel at ease. Our ride up to the seventh floor calms me somewhat and when we're deposited in my hallway, I'm shocked to find Bennett dressed in a suit and tie, looking dashing leaning against my doorjamb.

"What took you two so long?" He smirks, his eyes darkened resembling a mossy field glistening with mischief, but the concern hangs around us like a flightless balloon.

"It was ten goddamn minutes, Bennett."

All Carter gets is a chuckle, as I unlock the door and step inside. The apartment is quiet and dark. Flicking the switch beside the door, the living room illuminates with a dim light and we all shuffle into the open area. "Look, I'll be okay. I really don't—"

"You're not staying alone, Ella. That's final. No arguments." Bennett's not taking no for an answer, so I relent. I don't want to fight or argue. All I need is my medication and sleep.

"You'll be fine. I'll be back as soon as I can," Carter murmurs and I can't help smiling at his affection.

My gaze flits to Bennett and I watch him shrug out of his jacket. His shoulders are broad, sexy, and I can tell there's muscle under the crisp white material. How can I have two beautiful men wanting to dote on me like this? It doesn't make sense.

"I'll be right here, Cart," he tells his best friend, then turns his green eyes to me. "I'm right here all night," he assures me while getting comfortable on the sofa.

"Can I get you a drink or something?" I offer, and the salacious smile I'm met with tells me the *and something* caught his attention.

"Maybe later. Carter, I've got it." Deep green meets sapphire and something passes between the men that I can't read. Then Carter nods and cups my face in his hands.

"I won't be long." He plants a gentle kiss on my lips and leaves.

"I'm going to get changed. I'll be back in a sec," I tell my boss, who seems comfortable on my sofa.

Bennett nods and I can feel the heat of his gaze on me as I head into my bedroom. The memory of the card and snow globe assault me. I make quick work of changing into a pair of sweatpants and a baggy T-shirt. As soon as I'm back in the living room I allow the calm that Bennett offers to blanket me.

"Come here, honey. I don't bite… Hard." He chuckles playfully and I nestle in the crook of his arm.

"Isn't this strange for you? I'm your employee," I mumble into the spicy scent of his shirt. His arm tightens, as if he doesn't want me far.

"No. It's not strange. You're under my protection, as long as you're here, working for me. You know, Carter and I have grown to care for you," he tells me, his arms tightening their hold. "We'd do anything to protect you." His promise lifts the sadness and leaves a heavy fog of exhaustion that settles on my droopy eyelids and I allow sleep to come.

"Snowflake, come here." He's not drunk today. Maybe he won't hurt me.

Stepping into the living room, I find him sitting at the dinner table with pages spread out in front of him. When I near him, I realize he's got my diary pages which have been torn out of the book.

"What the fuck is this?" He points to my words and fear grips my neck, threatening to suffocate me.

"It's nothing. I promise." I can tell he's livid by the redness blotching his face. I can't do this again. Last night was too much and now I'm terrified of what he might do. I spent the day with excruciating pain between my legs. The boy I used to like, Jeremy, said hello to me today, but I couldn't even look at him. My fear has become unbearable

and the thought of anyone touching me makes me retch.

"Nothing? You whoring yourself out to the boys at school?" The papers go flying in his fit of rage as he pushes up from the chair. It drops with a loud thud that makes me jump.

"No! I helped a classmate with homework." Tears threaten, and as much as I don't want him to see me cry, I can't stop them from falling. He's going to hurt me again. I wish I could leave, run away where nobody can find me.

"Bend over this fucking table now." He points to the dinner table where I usually have my meals and the thought of what he'll do to me on there makes me sick to my stomach. Fear knots in my belly and I look into his cold gray eyes. There's no feeling in them, no emotion. Just the sick fascination with me. "Snowflake, if you don't fucking do it, I'll make you do it. Do you want me to make you do it?"

Shaking my head, I bend over the table, like he asked.

I pray that my mother will walk in. I pray, but no God can save me. There is no God because if there were, men like this wouldn't exist. My school skirt gets lifted and my panties are ripped from my hips. The burn on my skin causes more tears to fall and I hate that I'm so weak.

If I were facing him, maybe I could claw at him, bite him, or something. A loud swat on my ass has me yelping, which is my first mistake.

"If you don't shut up, you'll get your filthy panties stuffed in your fucking mouth."

I nod as he presses my face to the table.

"So you like being a whore? Don't you know I fucking own your cunt? No man will ever want you because you're broken. So I suggest you get the idea of love out of your fucking mind."

Another swat on my bare skin has me crying out, which is my second mistake. I watch him take the pages from my diary and crumple them up, stuffing them into my mouth.

I can't move as his body presses me down onto the hardwood.

"You make me feel good, Snowflake. You're not so white and pure, though, are you?"

I can feel his erection pushing into my ass.

"You're going to learn that you're fucking worthless."

The sound of his zipper echoes through the room.

I am strong. I am strong. I am strong.

Suddenly, pain I have never known before ignites and burns me from the inside out. My body feels as if it's been ripped in half. Broken. I am broken. My screams are muffled by the pages of my diary. By the words that kept me safe. Now they're the ones that torment me.

"That's it. Take me. You're so tight. I wanted this little ass for a long time." He grunts as he ploughs into me. Driving deeper and harder and faster. My mind hides, my body aches, and my soul… that was lost a long time ago.

I know I'll never be the same again.

"Ella…"

"Ella!"

Bolting up, I stare into Bennett's eyes.

"What? Where am I?" Glancing around, I see the familiar bedroom. My bedroom. He must have brought me in here when I fell asleep.

"You're in your apartment. I stayed because Carter is at the charity event." Bennett's expression is one of confusion. "You were screaming." He slips onto the bed beside me.

It's only when he reaches for me do I flinch. I know he won't hurt me, but the nightmare is still vivid in my mind, rearing its ugly head, reminding me I'm a used little girl.

"What happened, Ella?" He's staring at me and I know that look. There's determination in his eyes and I know I'm going to have to try and explain.

"It's a long—"

"Don't give me a shit excuse, honey. I want the truth. There's no way you're fine after what I heard when you had that nightmare moments ago."

I pull my legs up and wrap my arms around them. My heart thuds against my chest because this is the first time in my life that I'm about to tell someone what happened to me.

"Please, Ella, trust me." His eyes hold nothing but sincerity. I haven't known him for that long, but something about Bennett Ainsworth sets me at ease.

"Did Carter tell you about the box I got at dinner?"

He nods, waiting for me to continue.

"The snow globe is… it's… was a gift." Dropping my gaze to the sheet, I inhale deeply, needing to center my emotions. "My stepfather… I was sixteen and he bought me a snow globe." Tears burn behind my eyelids and I have to swallow past the lump in my throat.

"Ella…"

"I was sixteen when he pushed it inside me, Bennett." The words tumble out, and once they are, they hang like lead weights in the air. The room feels as if it's a shoebox, but when I glance at Bennett I don't find disgust but sadness. "He started abusing me…" Swiping my hand across my cheeks to wipe my tears that are now streaming down my face, I look away. Guilt. Shame. Fear. All these emotions fight and claw their way through me.

My body is shaking and I can't continue. He places a hand on my knee, which causes me to start, but I can't bring myself to look at him.

"I was… it was… two years before I left home."

"Fuck, sweetheart." He scoots closer, and I find myself relaxing into his embrace. "I'm right here. You're safe now. Please don't be scared of me. I would never hurt you."

I nod, but I'm not sure he notices.

"He took everything from me, Bennett. My innocence. My confidence. I felt so fragile in the dark every night. He invaded my mind, my body, and he blackened my soul." My voice cracks on the last word and that's when I let go. I've been holding more than six years of pain inside. Keeping it locked in a neat little box in the back of my mind, but as this man holds me, stroking my hair, my box breaks and everything comes pouring out.

There's nothing left for me to do but let go of years of pent-up emotion and let it all out.

"Shhh… I'm right here."

My tears soak his shirt and I grip the material like it's a lifeline keeping me afloat from the emotions that seem to want to pull me into the depths of despair and depression. I've just told him part of my past and he's still here, still holding me.

"Bennett." I pull back and stare at him. "I can't tell Carter, please. You have to promise me."

"Why? He cares for you, darling. I think you need to talk to him."

Shaking my head, I stare out of the window, taking in the inky sky and the twinkling stars. There's a sliver of the moon hanging in the darkness, not offering much light. "Bennett, you don't understand. I can't be with anyone. He wants something I can't give him."

"What if we both wanted you?"

His question jars me, stilling me in the spot. What?

"What do you mean?"

"Yes, Carter wants you, but so do I. I believe we can heal you, sweetheart. But we'll never force you to do something you don't want to. I've known Carter all my life and I trust him." He moves me then, allowing me to face him. "Be with us?" His voice is determined and confident.

"I-I don't know," I confess quietly. "Can you just hold me for now?"

He tugs me into his arms again and a feeling of security blankets me. It's the same feeling I get when I'm with Carter. "I'm here, love. I told you I'm not heading anywhere unless you ask me to."

I take in his scent for a moment, allowing his words to wash over me once more.

Carter wants you, but so do I. Be with us.

"Can we go to the living room? It's stuffy in here," I mumble into his shirt.

He nods, pulling me up and walking me to the other room. As soon as I sit on the sofa, he joins me. He's tentative when he reaches for my hand.

"So, the card and box you got at the dinner with Carter, it was him? Your stepfather?" His grip on my hands tightens and his gaze bores a hole into me, leaving me exposed.

"Yes..." Meeting his stare, I continue, "I got spooked. It's like he was there. I felt as if his eyes were leering at me like they used to. Before dinner, I walked into my bedroom and found the exact same snow globe in my bedroom. But, I haven't taken my medication in a few days. I-I didn't think."

"Medication?"

"When I turned nineteen I finally went to a doctor. I thought I was losing my mind. Hearing *him* everywhere. They told me it's auditory hallucinations from my trauma."

"Ella, look at me." His strong hands cup my face and I stare at him, waiting for him to tell me I'm crazy and my chest tightens. "I'm doing a background check. This has gone far enough. One call is all it will take. Don't worry. You've got me and Cart."

I nod. It's only when Bennett's thumbs swipe my cheeks do I realize I'm crying.

"Fuck, we need to tell Carter. He needs to know, Ella. Trust me. Look at me."

I drag my gaze to his and find honesty, sincerity, and understanding.

"Okay."

He pulls out his phone and hits dial. I can hear the ringing because he's sitting so close to me. The warmth of him bathes me and I can't help but shift closer. "Carter, get back here now."

I can only hear Bennett's side of the conversation. I can't imagine what Carter is thinking.

"She woke up from a nightmare and she needs you, us. There's something you need to know and it's best that she tells you."

When he hangs up, he plants a soft kiss on my forehead and I close my eyes. "Let me tell you about my best friend. He's an arsehole most days, but when he wants someone he won't stop until he gets them. Ella, I want to lean in right now and claim your lips, to make you forget everything." His words have my eyes snapping up and I cock my head to the side with my brows creasing into a frown.

"What—" My words are stopped by his lips. Shock vibrates through me, but when I place my hands on his chest and push, he relents. "You can't… I mean, I can't…"

He nods but as soon as he moves away, I miss his calm.

"I'll wait. We'll both wait, Ella, because you're ours," he whispers. He pushes up off the sofa to walk away, but I want him to offer me a reprieve from the tension and fear.

"Wait." My voice comes out rough with need, yearning.

He turns and eyes me warily.

"Please, just wait. I'm new to this, to talking and opening myself up to someone. And the two of you,

you're like a blanket of calm. You both offer me something I've never felt." My confession stills us both.

"Do you want us both, Ella?" he questions, our gazes clashing with desire. I can't find the words, so I nod. The downlights seem to illuminate his eyes. They're beautiful, sparkling like crystals. He smiles—it's a genuine one—and joins me on the sofa, pulling me into the crook of his arm. My eyes flutter closed and I hope my nightmares will stay away this time.

SIXTEEN

CARTER

"**B**AINES, GO STRAIGHT HOME. I'LL CALL YOU IF WE need anything, but at this time of the night, I doubt we will. Bennett is here, and he must have his car."

He nods and offers a smile. The man is my savior. "Yes, sir. I'll see you tomorrow. Good luck."

As I make my way up to the entrance, the doorman gives me a nod, allowing me to make my way to the lift. Pushing number seven, I wait for the doors to slide open to take me to her.

The ride up to the seventh floor is the longest journey, and by the time I reach her door, I'm anxious because of Bennett's call. My father wasn't impressed with me leaving early, but I don't give a shit. This is Ella. She's hurting and needs me and I'll be fucked if I let her wait.

I knock, then hear Bennett's voice from inside.

When the door opens he steps aside and I see her. It takes all my restraint not to rush to her. I don't want to scare her, but all I want to do is hold her.

She looks like she's been crying for days. "Carter." Her voice is croaky and she clears her throat, her eyes never leaving mine.

"Ella, I'm so fucking sorry I took so long. Are you okay?" My words fall like the walls I've hidden behind for so long. Bennett's hand on my shoulder startles me and I turn to him.

"Let's sit." He looks at home here and something tells me he's made a move already.

I settle on Ella's left, and Bennett on her right. She's sandwiched between us, the only place she belongs. There's no longer a choice in my mind. This is right. My heart aches seeing the pain in her expression, and all I want to do is protect her. When I look at Bennett, I see the same resolution in his eyes.

"Carter." Her soft, tentative voice drags my attention back to the reason I'm here. The incredibly beautiful woman beside me. Her eyes are shimmering with unshed tears. Seeing her in pain only makes me want to kill whoever hurt her. There's nothing for me to say until she tells me the truth.

"I'll start at the beginning; it will be better that way. When I was eighteen I ran away from home, from my life, and from my past. I've never had anyone who cared enough to ask why I didn't have any friends or why I was alone." She peers up at me shyly, and I realize I was the one who broke her barriers.

"We care, Ella."

She nods and places her hand on mine. When her skin touches mine, my intake of breath is sharp.

"I know that now. You see, when I was…" This time she breathes deeply and my gaze flits over to my best friend. He nods, but doesn't say anything. "When I was thirteen, my mother remarried." I remember her telling me her father passed away, but she never spoke of another man in her life.

"He was good to us… but… I…" Tears tumble down her cheeks and I can't stop myself. I reach out and swipe them from her pretty face. She's perfect even when she's crying. "It was my sixteenth birthday." She laughs wryly. It drips with pain, which seeps into my veins, darkening my heart because I have a feeling I know what's coming.

"He… I was… I mean, he took me…"

My vision blurs and I see red. Pushing up from the sofa, I hear an animalistic sound and I realize it's me growling. *Fucking arsehole!* I need to punch something. I need to fucking break something, someone, with my bare fucking hands.

"Carter, sit down."

Pivoting, I glare at my best friend. He's right, I should let her get it out. I find my seat again, but my body is vibrating with fury.

I take her hands in mine, watching her submit to my touch. "Baby, I don't know what to say."

"The card and box. It was him..." Her body shudders, but she continues, "The first time he ever gave me a snow globe was a few months after my birthday."

I have to frown at this and her eyes find mine.

"It was a snow globe with Buckingham Palace and a red bus inside."

"I don't understand, baby."

"That night he showed me what he wanted to do with it." Her gaze implores me to understand and when I do, bile rises in my throat, burning like a poison threatening to kill me.

"Ella."

"He fucked me with it." Her voice breaks on the

words and I don't resist pulling her body against mine.

Anger heats my blood and I can't fucking see straight. I've been angry before. Hell, I've been furious with people, but this is a whole different type of rage that's coursing through me.

Her body so pliable against mine makes me want to hold her forever. My gaze meets Bennett's and I can see the pain he feels for her. He cares about her as much as I do. When I first saw her, I knew she'd be different. She's the one for us.

"Baby, you don't—"

"I woke from a nightmare earlier, and Bennett asked me about it. So now you both know my dark secret." The woman I love was hurt and violated by a sick bastard who's out there fucking with her head.

"We'll find him, baby. I promise you." Meeting Bennett's stare, he nods and I know this fucker will not survive the wrath of me and my best friend.

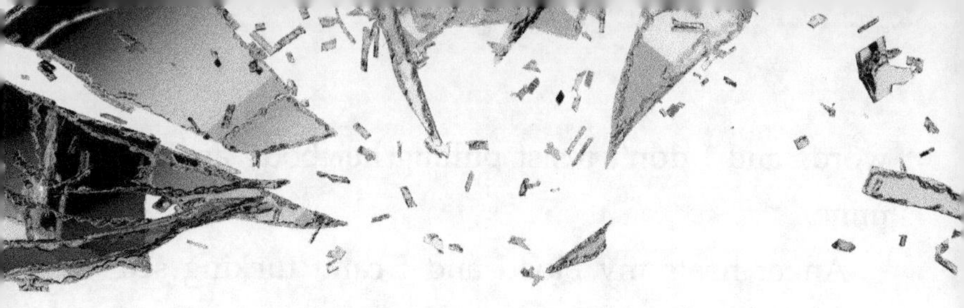

SEVENTEEN

ELLA

H
E SITS ABSOLUTELY STILL, BUT I KNOW THERE'S A silent conversation going on between the two men who've come to mean more to me than anyone ever has. There's a vow in Carter's words that's unsaid but known by me and Bennett. He'll kill for me.

The sooner Charles is found, I know I'll be okay. Freedom is something that's always been elusive to me, but with both men fighting for me, there's just an inkling I might make it through. Right now, though, all I want to do is be cocooned between these two incredible men.

The broken girl. The tainted whore.

I want them both.

Does that make me a bad person? No.

Does that make me a slut? No.

Does that mean I'm finally fixed? Maybe.

The first thing I know I need to do is find a psychologist who can assess me once more. This time there aren't any hallucinations. He really has found me. There aren't any vivid dreams or morbid thoughts, only real-life memories.

I curl up and they both wrap their arms around me. Now they both know who I am and what I've come from. My sordid past is out in the open and they haven't run. They're both here and for the first time in years I feel like a woman who's desired for the right reasons.

"Princess."

I turn to Bennett. His gaze is soft, yet commanding.

"Princess."

My gaze flits to Carter. He looks as if he wants to devour me. My head is spinning, like I'm on a carnival ride and out of control.

"Let me in. Don't worry. I'll find him and kill him with my bare fucking hands, but don't push me away. Please?"

My heart leaps at his sincere promise. I want Carter, there's no doubt in my mind, but I turn to Bennett and realize I want him too.

I nod. I agree. Nothing can stop my need for them.

"Sleep now. We'll talk after you've had some rest."

My eyes close and I feel safe, more so than I ever have in my entire life.

Rolling over, I find a warm hand on my hip and one on my arm. Cracking my eyes, finding the source of the heat cocooning me and after my confession, I can't help smiling. Two incredibly beautiful men are holding me. "How long was I asleep?" I ask, my voice groggy with sleep.

"About an hour," Bennett answers with a smirk, his gaze roving over me like a hungry lion.

Pushing up, I settle between them, finding myself relaxed and calm.

"Can I have one?" I gesture to the whisky.

Carter hands me his glass, which I take gratefully and down the strong liquid in a long gulp. As it burns its way down, my mind reels with the emotions warring inside me. Unrestrained desire and the unbidden ache between my legs tell me I'm just a normal woman, with ordinary needs.

Glancing between the two, I know that if I were

forced to choose, I couldn't. *Are these emotions that normal people experience? What they crave?* Carter trails a featherlight touch down my arm, causing me to tremble.

Bennett copies the action on my other arm and the pleasure that coils deep in my core is foreign but wanted. It's unbelievable for me to know safety with a man. Most won't understand it. But if you've been broken so many times, for so long, there's no doubt you'd feel the same. My fragile innocence was stolen in a few seconds, but I think somehow, both Bennett and Carter may be able to heal the shattered pieces of me.

"Ella, do you trust us?" My eyes find the blue shimmer of Carter's and I nod.

He leans in and kisses me tentatively, sweetly.

It's passionate, not filthy.

It's gentle, yet demanding.

And I have a feeling he's holding back. In fact, I know he is.

Bennett's hands stroke my back, gripping my hips in a firm grasp. He tugs me against him, my back to his solid chest. A small shiver of anticipation shoots through me as his heat encapsulates me. "Ella, close your eyes, darling." His deep rumble vibrates against my body from behind and my pussy pulses. They want to show me pleasure, something I've never allowed myself to experience.

"I'm not… I—"

"Shh, trust us, darling."

I stare into those sea storm eyes that implore me to let go. They glint with desire like sunrays warming me. With Carter in front of me and Bennett behind me, my body is completely cocooned between them. The T-shirt I'm wearing slips off my shoulders so slowly I hardly notice. Only when Bennett's warm lips come into contact with my skin does my body tremble with need and desire that's tightened my core deliciously.

"Close your eyes, Ella, I'm right here. I promise." His words are a whisper, barely audible, but I feel them right down to my soul.

My eyes flutter closed and warm fingers trace the curve of my neck, the outline of my lips, and the sensitive skin behind my ear. Hot breath tantalizes me from the soft kisses my boss plants on my shoulders, one after the other. Every inch of my skin is prickling, tingling, thrumming. While Carter focuses on my mouth, his lips whisper over mine, down to my jaw and to the swell of my breasts.

Hot, wet, and hungry.

He suckles my skin into his mouth, allowing his teeth to graze the flesh, and I'm about to explode. A volcano rumbling with molten lava swirls in my stomach. Traveling down to my core and my panties are soaked with arousal for not one man but two.

"I'm going to slip your bra off, Ella." Carter's deep voice in my ear sends an erotic shiver through me and I nod. The thin straps of silk slide down my shoulders and the material lands on the floor with a gentle whoosh. "Fuck." His growl has me opening my eyes, and when my gaze meets his, they're turbulent.

"Is something wrong?" I question, frowning at him.

"You're perfect," Bennett hums against me as his hands find my full breasts. His fingers tweak and tug on my nipples and they harden to tight peaks. When he drops his hands, Carter's mouth laves at the one bud, taunting and teasing it. His teeth graze over the pebbled peak, causing me to whimper and moan. My head drops back and Bennett is there.

His lips find mine in a deep, passionate kiss, as he traces the seam of my mouth, seeking entrance, and I let him have it. Our tongues dance in an erotic tumble. The vibration in his chest has electricity shooting through me.

"Let us show you pleasure, baby. Trust us," Carter urges me with a ferocious growl.

Breaking the kiss, I look up at one of the men who broke my walls down. Who's been relentless in his pursuit.

"I'll try." My voice is thick with emotion. There's no fear, only lust.

"My sweet Princess," he murmurs and never in my life has a nickname made me feel more powerful. I'm in charge. They're not taking, they're giving. As that realization settles in my mind, I feel off-kilter. I'm on the edge of a cliff and I'm about to leap. But I won't fall. With Bennett and Carter, I'll fly.

"Let's get more comfortable." Bennett scoops me up and turns toward my bedroom.

My feelings for both these men are spiraling inside me, a storm brewing. It's about to rain down with more passion than I've ever felt and I don't know how I'll handle it, but I'm willing to try.

He places me on the bed, and I watch as they unbutton their shirts. I can't hide the smile that plays on my lips. *How have I found myself here?* Watching two incredibly gorgeous men strip down to nothing but tight black boxer briefs with thick hard bulges that are solid steel for me. Both want to take me and own me.

"See something you like, Princess?" Carter's overconfident smirk has my heart racing, and when I glance at Bennett, his cocky grin has my blood thrumming.

"I do actually. I see two somethings I like. Now I wonder if they're just going to stand there and watch me, or are they going to do something about it." I don't know where my courage comes from, but my hand drops between my thighs and when I part my legs I stroke the thin lace material. My clit is throbbing, needing attention. Even though I've never been with a man and found pleasure, I've managed by myself.

Both sets of eyes devour me. They're glued to the show I put on for them and I feel like a queen ruling an army.

"Open those beautiful legs wider, sweetheart." The green-eyed god growls and I do. I obey him because the way he's looking at me is not filthy, demeaning, or wrong. It's affectionate, lustful, and hungry.

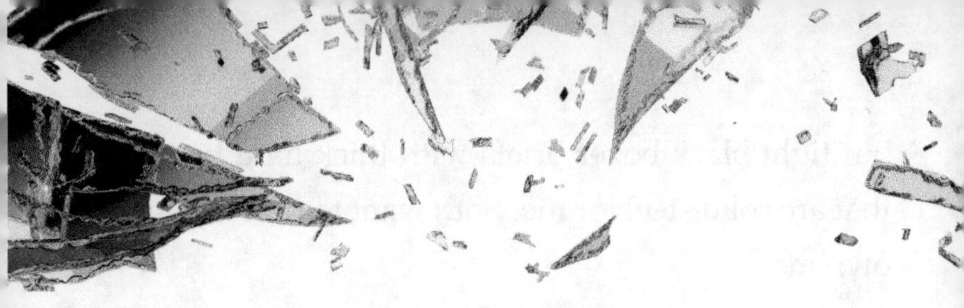

EIGHTEEN

BENNETT

STANDING BESIDE MY BEST FRIEND IN MY UNDERWEAR while the woman we're falling for strokes her perfect little pussy is like a dream come true. I've never wanted love, but this right here makes me realize I may not have wanted it, but it's found me.

Kneeling on the bed on her right, Carter kneels on her left. He replaces her hand with his and I watch his expression change from calm to explosive.

"Fuck, Ella, you're soaked," he grunts out through clenched teeth as he strokes her gently. Her moans filter through the haze of lust and I focus my attention on her beautiful tits. They're full and heavy. Her pert nipples are dark, beautiful, and hard.

My mouth drops to one while I tweak and tease the other. Carter drops to his knees and her legs open for him instinctively. I watch as he tugs the knickers down her slender legs. Once they're off, her sweet scent of arousal has me inhaling deeply, reveling in her. Fuck, this woman could bring down armies.

When his mouth closes in on her pussy, I bite down on her nipple, not to hurt her, but to show her that pain can equal pleasure. Her moans echo through the room. It's like a melody of the sweetest song and I'd like to have it on repeat as her body convulses in an orgasm.

"Oh God, ohhh… ohhhh…." She mewls like a kitten as we devour her. My cock is hard, painfully so, and all I want to do is slide into her tight heat. To feel her pulse around me. But we need to take this slow.

Watching him feast on her wet cunt almost undoes me and I have to focus on her eyes fluttering and her plump lips that are parted as she whimpers.

I reach up, stroking the smooth skin of her cheeks, and goosebumps dot every inch of her. For her to find pleasure, with not just one man but two is astonishing. Her body bows and an orgasm wracks through her. Shivers and trembles, moans and hisses echo around us.

Her thighs quake on either side of Carter's face and I suck her nipple into my mouth, flicking it with my tongue as she grips my hair with one hand and his with the other.

The sounds she makes when she comes apart are an aphrodisiac because I need to be inside her.

"Carter," I bite out his name, my voice laced with lust, and when his eyes meet mine, he nods. I waste no time in pushing my boxers down. Her amethyst eyes shimmer as they flit between me and him. I watch her tongue dart out and she licks her lips like she's about to feast on a buffet.

"I'm going to fuck you, Princess, and I want you to suck Bennett's cock, okay?" Carter's voice is a growl laced with lust and I smirk.

She nods slowly while her wide eyes watch him sheath himself. As soon as the tip of his cock comes into contact with her core, she freezes. Her body goes rigid and her eyes shut tight.

"Open your eyes. Look at me." His order is commanding and I know he's got to be stern or she'll always be afraid. Her submissive nature has her opening those amethyst gems, latching onto his movements.

It's torture watching him slide into her. She

must be tight because he goes so slow. My eyes are transfixed on the sight of them connecting, so I don't notice her mouth enveloping my thick, hard shaft. It's only when her lips wrap around the crown do I groan as pleasure rips violently through me.

Her mouth is warm and wet and it's taking all my restraint not to be too rough or fuck her beautiful face because I want to. God, do I want to.

"Fuck, Ella, you're going to suck my fucking soul out through my dick it feels so good."

She's amazing at giving head. Her tongue swirls around the shaft and when Carter is fully seated inside her, she hums her approval, sending shockwaves through my body.

"Fucking hell, you're so tight, my sweet girl," he murmurs in awe. His restraint is slipping as he pulls out and plunges back in with such careful movements I'm amazed. Staring at my best friend, I watch his head drop back in pleasure. We time our movements as we take Ella to heights she's never ever dreamed of. She hums around my cock again and I fight back the release tingling through every nerve in my body.

"Ella, you need to—" My words are cut off when Carter reaches for her clit and rubs slow circles around it, sending her spiraling over the edge, dragging me along the precipice as a release hits me suddenly and jets of hot cum shoot down her throat. She greedily swallows every fucking drop and my knees go weak as I watch her devour me. The ache to fuck her is renewed and I glance at my best friend, telling him with my eyes.

We stare at each other for a while before he nods. I want this woman to come with my cock buried so deep inside her she'll forget her own fucking name. Leaning in, I plant a soft kiss on her lips.

"We're going to take a shower now."

She smiles and nods. The pleasure she's just experienced is new to her and her eyes glisten.

I push off the bed and leave her with Carter. In the bathroom, I turn on the multi-head shower and glance in the mirror. My hair is disheveled and the smirk on my face is of unadulterated lust. I know what he's got running through his mind. We're going to double team her and I know for a fact her dirty side will come out to play.

The bathroom steams up quickly. The soft padding of bare feet heading toward me causes my heart rate to spike. When I turn to the entrance, I find the dark-haired temptress who just sucked my dick like she was born to do it.

"The shower is ready. Are you?" I offer her a wicked smile and she blushes, so innocent, but when her eyes find mine there's something sexy and dirty flickering in them. The little tigress has come out to play.

NINETEEN

ELLA

Two men. Two men. Two men.

My mind can't fathom it.

I feel like a virgin heading off to be sacrificed. The orgasm that tore through me only moments before has my knees wobbly and my skin prickling. When Carter slid into me, I froze for a moment, my eyes shut so tight I didn't want it to happen, but he commanded me.

He ordered me to look at him and when my gaze met his, I waited for the dark thoughts and fear to close in around me, but they faded. He was my anchor. I felt all the affection, possessiveness, and lust as he took me. He was gentle, slow, and I know it must have been difficult for him to restrain himself.

As we enter the bathroom, Bennett's heated gaze travels from my hair down to my toes. It's so slow and it feels as if he's set me alight and the flames lick over my skin, scorching every inch of me.

"Are you okay, Princess? You can say no at any time." Carter's domineering manner is subdued, and I wonder if he's worried I'm about to run.

I turn in his arms and plant a soft kiss on his cheek. His hands drift to my ass and he squeezes the cheeks in his large, smooth hands. Lifting me, he allows my legs to wrap around his taut waist as he stalks into the large shower.

Once the spray hits us both, he lets me down to my feet. As Bennett steps closer toward us, a memory assaults me. I recall the moment I first walked into the bathroom, I fantasized the stranger from the airport dropping his crisp white shirt on the tiles before we both stepped into the shower and made love under the spray. It was also that moment I wondered if the shower would fit three. A giggle escapes my lips and both men stare at me.

"You know, having a woman giggle while I'm naked isn't my idea of fun." Bennett chuckles as I meet his affectionate gaze.

"There's nothing to laugh about here," I whisper, trailing a finger over his chiseled abs, gripping his hardened erection in my hand. His eyes narrow.

He closes the distance between us. The three of us are under the heated cascade. Wet and slippery. Anticipation sets my skin alight. There's a heaviness in my stomach, tightening with want.

My pussy quivers around nothing. I want to feel them inside me again. The ache Carter fucked away moments ago is back with a vengeance. Both men step forward, blanketing me in their warmth and safety.

Bennett's hands grip my hips and Carter in turn cups my face. With a soft kiss landing on my lips, he turns me to face his best friend. Sandwiched between two alpha males is a heady feeling. I'd compare it to being drunk, that soft fizzle that tingles through you from the top of your head and heats its way down to your toes.

I feared for so long and now that I'm here panic is the last thing on my mind.

Bennett stares at me. He doesn't look jealous at all and I realize he wanted this. They both did.

Even though I've just had his cock in my mouth, it feels more intimate kissing him, his tongue teasing mine. Carter wraps his arms around my waist, with one hand splayed on my stomach. His other reaches for my pussy. When he finds it dripping a deep, guttural growl rumbles through his chest.

"You're drenched again, Princess. Is your pussy needy, baby?" His words have my core clenching around his fingers. Tightening, pulling them deeper into my body. "Does my beautiful girl want two cocks?" he murmurs, skating his fingers over the lips of my core. He plants a kiss on the wet skin of my shoulder.

"Please…" I beg.

I. Fucking. Beg.

I glance up under wet lashes at Bennett and offer a shy smile as he growls. "I'm taking that sweet arse, sweetheart, and you'll never forget it." His words send panic racing through me at the thought of him inside that part of my body. Both men notice me freeze.

"Look at me, Ella." Carter's deep baritone cloaks me and I drag my worried gaze to his. "Feel me, feel Bennett. You're safe," he murmurs as two sets of hands stroke, hold, and grip me in their safety.

They're both similar height, and a few inches taller than me, which makes me stare up at them. Carter's lips find mine and he lifts me against his body again. I wrap my legs around his waist and the tip of his cock teases my pussy. I'm wet, slick with desire, and needy for him to fill me.

"Shit, I need a—"

"It's okay, I'm safe," I whisper. Our gazes meet in a standoff and I offer a swift nod, telling him I want him inside me with no barriers. Just us. Skin on skin.

That must be all he needed because he moves. His hips roll, but they're controlled as he slides me down his shaft and once he's fully seated, my body tenses.

"Jesus, Ella," he grunts, "your greedy, little pussy better stop trying to milk my cock dry, because I'm in fucking charge and this time you're going drench my cock at least twice in your sweet juices before either of us fills you with cum."

I whimper at the dirty words. The naughty promises he utters.

"Now grip my fucking shoulders, because we're going to own you." His order is filthy, purely sinful, but I love every syllable. A devilish smirk curls his full lips. It's sexy as hell and I twine my arms around his neck. I know I'm in for an intense ride.

His best friend presses his chest against my back, and when his fingers find the tight forbidden hole I gasp in shock. "Relax, darling, concentrate on

Carter," Bennett assures me. His fingers tease my back entrance gently. Then he slides one finger into to me, I pant and claw at the man holding me up. Another hand wraps around me and between us Bennett's fingers tease my clit.

"Sweet Jesus, Ella, your pussy is like a vice. You feel so fucking good on my cock." My blue-eyed god growls and I smile. We move in unison, fingers and cock filling me, and I'm flying.

Soaring. Aching. Moaning. Screaming.

I've never felt so full. I've never had so much pleasure bestowed on my body. My head falls back as my orgasm tightens in my lower stomach. A slow, sensual sensation starts from the roots of my hair, trailing white hot pleasure—mingled with a bite of pain—lower and lower until it reaches my spine. It sizzles down to my tailbone, and it gathers, low and forceful in my womb. My toes curl. My pussy clamps down on the cock inside me and the two fingers probing me.

I'm hovering on the precipice of lust and desire between them.

It's erotic. It's addictive. It's perfect.

I need more.

"Bennett, please," I whimper as his digits scissor

me open, getting me ready, loose and gaping for his thick length.

He nudges my tight hole with the tip of his dick. It's wet and slippery and as Carter's teeth graze my nipples I relax and suddenly I'm impaled. Both men are inside me and it feels as if I'm hurtling down a cliff.

Sparks, fireworks, lightning. All three go off at the same time and my body convulses wildly around both men. My throat is raw from the loud screams they elicit, but they don't stop. He's keeping his promise. I'll find another release between them.

Like a thunder storm, it moves slow and threateningly through the dark sky. As if I'm watching it, I feel the impending rumble in the distance. That's how my orgasm teases. I know when it hits, it'll be fit for heaven. I'm in the clouds and my body is weightless. They move in a rhythm that rocks me and lulls away any fear or panic.

"Fuck, you're tight, darling."

"Jesus, baby, you're incredible."

I hear their words, but I can't respond because pleasure has overridden my mind and all I can do is whimper and moan. I don't know who's speaking, who's uttering beautiful words at me. My nails dig in and I cry out as an orgasm thunders through me.

"Please… God… fuck…" Unintelligible mumbles fall from my mouth.

"That's it, Ella. Pleasure. Feel it. Every fucking moment of it."

I think it's Carter because the voice strains in front of me. He's so deep inside me I feel him nudge my womb. Bennett slides out and slams back into me, while Carter drives his cock, deeper and harder. Faster and faster. They've created a rhythm. It's divine, it's unadulterated, and I feel another release close by.

"Please…"

Bennett leans in and his tongue trails over my neck to my jaw. When his mouth reaches my ear, his teeth bear down on my lobe, sending pleasured pain skittering over my skin.

"Open your eyes, Princess," the command comes from the man seated inside my pussy. I meet his gaze—hungry, desperate, and beautiful. He's perfect. "You feel this?" He slams into me and I nod. "You see me?"

Again, I acknowledge.

"This is me fucking you." Again and again he drives deep and furiously.

"You feel me, darling?" A deep rumble behind me steals my breath and I nod. "This is me fucking you." The exquisite pain has me teetering on the edge.

Memories are forgotten when fingers find my clit, circling it, sending me crashing, falling, tumbling into pleasure as sparks explode behind my eyelids. My body tenses and pulses.

"Fuck, I can't hold back, baby. I'm coming inside this perfect little arse." Bennett's growl echoes as my body loses all control. Carter's cock thickens and I know he's close.

"Look at me." Carter's command tugs me back to earth. His eyes melt into mine. "This is us, Ella. We fucking own this body." His release shudders through him and the heat of his seed bathes me, marks me, and I know without a doubt I'm theirs.

TWENTY

CARTER

HER BODY IS FLAWLESS. HER BEAUTY IS breathtaking. There was more intimacy between the three of us than I've ever experience before when Bennett and I shared a woman. I saw Bennett's eyes. He's falling. So am I. We connected, physically and mentally. She found her way into my mind when I first saw her, and now that we've claimed her body, she's woven herself into our hearts.

Bennett slips out of her and she shudders. Her whimper is fuel to me, the need to protect her is fierce. "Are you okay, sweetheart?" he questions, a mere whisper in her ear, and she nods languidly with a smile. "I'll be in the bedroom." He glances at me and our understanding is communicated easily.

As soon as he steps out of the shower, I meet her gaze. There are questions running rampant in her mind. I soften inside her. I want to keep us connected, but I need to see if she's okay.

"Ella, I need you to tell me how you feel. Be honest."

She smiles. It's small, sweet, and innocent. I let her feet down and her eyes meet mine. "I'm scared you're both going to leave." These are the first words that fall from her lips as she frowns. My heart leaps into my throat. "I hate how I feel because I'm strong and independent, but with you and Bennett…" Her words are confident but taper off. The water cools and her nipples harden as she shivers.

"Let's get out of the shower." I pull her into my embrace, turn off the taps, and we step into the bathroom. Reaching for one of her towels, I wrap her up, then find another towel, tying it around my waist. Her body seems small after what we've just done. Standing in front of her, I take both her hands in mine. "Ella, we meant what we said. We want you. Bennett and I, we wanted to show you pleasure. We needed to show you something. You don't have to be scared. Don't fear us. Don't push us away because we're not going anywhere."

She nods, but I wait. I can't force her to answer me. I can't force her to choose. It's up to her. She had to see pleasure comes from the touch of someone who cares. My best friend and I used to do this in college all the time, and I wouldn't trust anyone else with her or around her. But this time it's different. We both love her. We both want her. I know we can live a life together, the three of us. Ultimately, she needs to decide.

"Carter, this has been a long, strange day. What I just did in there"—she glances at the empty shower, then back at me—"having you and Bennett touch me, pleasure me, is all so new. For the first time in my life I feel like a woman." Her glistening eyes pierce me. They look through me, into the darkest parts of me, and they pick at the ugly and shine purity on them. I want her to look at me like that all the time.

There's a fragile innocence to her as she peeks up at me. A tangible sweetness that most women I've been with no longer possess.

"I don't feel like a whore." A tear escapes and rolls down her cheek.

I lean in and kiss it before it reaches her chin. Tasting her saltiness on my lips, I savor it. "You're not a whore. I never, ever want you to say that about yourself again. Do you understand me?"

She nods. My heart thuds in my chest, coming alive after years of being cold and dead. I want to fall at her feet and worship her because this woman has brought me to my knees.

I rise and pull her body against mine. She molds to me. Her pliable and submissive nature is like a drug. It makes me want to shoot up. To feel her in my veins, thrumming through my blood and giving oxygen to my heart.

I've been an arsehole my whole life. Given up on being a loving man. I've fucked women for fun, to hurt them, but with Ella it's different. I know her past. Now all I need to do is confess mine. If she can accept my mistakes, if she can look past the man I used to be, I know I can be good for her.

When we head into the bedroom, Bennett is dressed in his blue jeans. I glance at Ella and her cheeks are rosy as she takes in his tattoos. My best friend has incredible ink on his chest and shoulder and I know she thinks he's attractive.

"Hey sweetheart. You feeling okay?" he questions with his cocky smirk and she giggles.

"Yes. I'm…" She glances at me, then back at him. "I'm perfect."

"That you are, Princess." I plant a kiss on the top

of her head. She smells so sweet, I wish I could get a taste of her again, but I know she'll be sore and sleepy after what we just did.

He pulls her into his arms, murmuring in her ear, "You're utterly exquisite. I have to leave, but I'll be back tomorrow. Okay?"

She nods in agreement.

"Sweet dreams, my sweetheart."

He's always been the romantic one. Caring and loving.

"I'm going to head out. There's a meeting early tomorrow morning with some of my guys. I'll let you know when I have any information."

They're going to find that fucker and I'll be the one to bring him justice. I'll rain down on that arsehole like a fucking thunderstorm, and when I'm done, he'll beg to be put in prison.

I glance at my girl and her eyes are droopy. Walking her to the bed, I sit her down and kneel. "I'm going to walk Bennett out. Lie down and I'll be back in a sec."

She nods and smiles. Before we leave the room, she calls out to my best friend. We both turn and she leans up.

"Thank you, for… I mean…"

"That's the first of many, Ella." He smirks confidently.

When we reach the living room, I stop at the door and look at the man who's like a brother to me.

"Are you sure about this, Cart? I know you love her." His words ring true.

"And you do too," I offer.

He nods. "I do."

"You're the only man I'd ever share her with. She needs you as much as she does me. We always joked about taking a trinity pact. Three hearts. Three bodies. One soul," I murmur quietly.

He nods, acknowledging my words. This is what she needs, and there's nothing I wouldn't do for her.

"I want this," he murmurs. He grips the nape of my neck, pulling me into his mouth as we share a heated kiss. "And next time, I'll be taking you and her." It's a vow and I know he'll make good on it. There's only been a handful of times we've been with each other in that way, but after the way his tongue snaked into my mouth, I know I want him as much as I do her. He turns and opens the door, but before he walks out, he glances at me again. "See you later." And then he's gone.

Before we can talk to her later about the pact we

made, I need to come clean. To tell her the reason I was forced to come back to London by my father. Anxiety thrums through my veins. Confessing my past to anyone is not something I want to do, especially someone I care about. I'm not proud of any of it.

Ella has been through so much and I don't want to upset her. Fuck, I don't want to lose her. But if she wants this, she'll have to know. Making my decision to tell her in the morning, I head back into the bedroom and find her asleep, curled into a ball, wrapped in a blanket. Her long hair is fanned behind her on the pillow. She looks like an angel.

Padding forward, I sit on the bed and stare at her. Her long lashes flutter open and she smiles when she sees me. "Hey," she murmurs and I reach forward and trace her cheek with my fingers.

"Hi, beautiful." As soon as my skin touches hers there's a spark between us and I never want to stop touching her. "Are you feeling okay? Are you sore?"

"A little bit, but it's a good pain. I want to thank you…" Her words trail off and her gaze drops to where my hand is linked with hers.

"For?" I question her with a frown. A soft rosy blush spreads from her cheeks to her chest. She's so beautiful.

"For everything. For making me feel again. Giving me pleasure I never felt before. And for Bennett…" Her words trickle into nothing. Her voice is like a soft rain cooling me after a hot day. Nobody has ever been able to disarm me with a single glance, a whimper, or a touch. But she does.

I reach for her chin, lifting it with my index finger, allowing her gaze to flicker up to mine. The silence in her bedroom is deafening, but the world falls away as we stare at each other.

"The princes claim their princess," I whisper in awe of her. Planting a soft kiss on her lips, I savor the taste of her. "You've helped me more than you know. You've turned a monster into a man."

"You're no monster, Carter." Her whispered response hits me in the chest where my heart beats erratically.

"Sleep now," I order and she obeys. Her eyes flutter closed and silence settles around us. I need to tell her what I was forced to do, what my father told me was right. If she can see past that and accept me as I am, then I know it will be okay.

TWENTY ONE

ELLA

SUNLIGHT STREAMS THROUGH THE BLINDS, THE HEAT of it nothing like the warmth from the body behind me. Smooth skin, toned muscles, and an arm that lies heavy on my hip makes me smile. As soon as I roll over, I find those sparkling eyes watching me.

"How long have you been awake?" My words are raspy and heavy with sleep. The side of his lip lifts into a smirk that sets my body ablaze.

"A little while," he murmurs.

"And you've been watching me all this time?"

He nods but doesn't respond. His hand trails from my hip, down to my thigh.

"Open." A one-word command I obey easily.

My legs splay. His fingers tease their way to my sensitive inner thigh. Each featherlight touch is electric, as if he's flicking a switch on every nerve in my body. It courses through me, heating my blood, tightening my core.

When he reaches my pussy, he strokes me reverently, gently, and delicately. Like I'll break if he presses just an inch harder. His thumb finds my clit and it thrums as he circles it, causing arousal to drench my pussy. My hips buck, needing it harder, needing it faster, aching to feel the pained pleasure he's so good at doling out.

"Carter, please?"

My plea goes unanswered. His concentration is not on my face but rather on the slick flesh between my legs. Steadily, he drives two fingers into me, with a slow precision that has me gripping the sheets.

"All in due time, Princess. I want to watch you unravel and fly," he coos—deep, seductive, dripping with desire. He strums me like an instrument, drawing my orgasm, which is bearing down on me from the depths of my body, from my heart and soul.

He pumps into me, in, out, in, out. The soft sounds of my arousal echo around me. The growl in his chest and the whimpers that fall from my lips are like a concerto, playing around us in perfect harmony. When his hand moves faster, fucking me like I need him to, my toes curl and my knuckles are painfully taut as I grip the sheet below me.

"Fly for me. Come on my hand and soak my fingers with those sweet juices I want to devour." His words send me reeling, soaring, and I'm floating into nothing. Everything tightens and his thumb presses on my clit as he crooks his fingers inside me. Light, darkness, bliss.

When my eyes flutter open, he's watching me intently, his fingers in his mouth, licking the glistening juice from each digit. "Carter—"

"I could get high on your taste alone, baby," he murmurs and kisses me, allowing me to taste myself on his lips, tongue, and I revel in everything he's giving me.

Stepping into the kitchen, I'm dressed in a pair of jeans and a big, white woolen jumper. Carter sets a plate in front of me and a large mug of coffee.

"Wow, what did I do to deserve this?" I giggle, digging into the toast and scrambled egg.

"Well, actually, there's something we need to talk about. You've told me your past, your demons.

Now… there's something I need to explain before we… before you… I mean…"

I reach out for his hand and he looks up at me. Every time we touch there's an inexplicable connection. Like a current running through us and I feel as if I'm alive, like I'm real. Dropping my fork, I slip from the stool and round the counter. He pulls me into his frame, calming the erratic beating of my heart.

We walk toward the sofa and settle comfortably. His eyes hold secrets, those he's about to spill, but I don't want him to worry. I'm not going anywhere.

"Carter—"

"Ella, when I was nineteen, I made a mistake. One that could have changed the course of my life." His gaze drops and I can tell this is difficult for him to admit. My heart aches for him, to hold him, but I don't interrupt. "My father stepped in and helped me, but he never let me forget it. It's the worst thing I've ever let happen and I need you to know the truth. Before you choose to be with us."

"You were serious about all three of us in a relationship?" I did think he was joking, but from the way he's looking at me, there's no doubt he was deadly serious.

"We are. If you can handle both of us wanting you, caring for you."

My heart thuds in my chest, agreeing to what he's offering, and I find myself nodding without doubt.

He smiles. It's the bright one that lights up the room. "Then you need to know what lies in my past. I was seeing a girl in college. Her name was Sadie. It wasn't serious. We'd just hook up. It was about two months after I'd first met her when she came to me in tears. She was pregnant. I didn't believe her at first, but when she told me how far along she was, I figured it had to me mine." As soon as the words are out of his mouth they hang in the air just out of reach, taunting me. "I asked for a paternity test when the time came because when I told her I wasn't ready for that kind of responsibility, she demanded money. I thought that was her ploy, so I went to Dad."

His face is etched with pain and fear, and I realize he's worried I'm going to walk away.

"You have a child?" I question gently, reaching for his hand and slipping it into mine. When he shakes his head my heart gallops and my stomach drops. My brows crease into a frown as I stare at him.

"My father paid her, one million dollars to get rid of it." His mouth purses into a grim line, but he doesn't meet my gaze. I know why. He's ashamed. It's written all over his face. Guilt is a terrible emotion to live with for so long, and it's been eating at him all these years.

"And did she?" I question.

He nods slowly and the words that were hanging in the air pop, dropping like lead weights. It resounds in my ears and I realize it's my heart hammering.

"I'm sorry."

His gaze snaps up to mine. "You shouldn't be sorry, Ella. When I saw her after the fact, she told me she'd never wanted a child but needed money to get out of all her student loans and debt. She told me I was an easy target. She took the money and loved every moment of being free of the burden of being a mother."

"Is she still a part of your life, Carter?"

"No. I wanted to tell you because it should come from me, no one else. There's nothing to be jealous about. I spoke to Bennett and he's agreed that if you decide to do this, it's the three of us. Together."

He doesn't say anything more and I wonder

if I should say something. Do I console him? I'm not angry. I can't be a hypocrite and judge him on something in his past. Mine is littered with violence and heartache.

"She's a mistake that happened so many years ago. I fucked up and I moved on. Nothing about her makes me want her, but when I look at you, I know in my heart I want everything with you. I want us." He pulls me against him affectionately.

"Carter, I'm—"

"I'm not prepared to lose you." His tone is adamant, confident in what he wants, and our gazes lock in a heated stare. His words are a salve to the open wounds in my heart and mind. I want to climb inside him. I want to find myself again. "Come on, eat your breakfast. I think we need to spend some time together."

"I have work today."

"Bennett will join us. You need a day to recoup and it will give you time to see how things would be between the three of us."

"Are you two? I mean…"

"We've been together a few times, yes," he answers my unasked question with honesty. That's what I love about them. Both Bennett and Carter tell me what's on their mind. There aren't any games behind their words.

"Wow."

"We'll play tonight. Would you like to see us together?"

I never thought I'd be turned on seeing two men together, but the thought of him and Bennett causes my nipples to harden. "Yes." I find myself responding because I do. I'd love to see it. "And as much as I'd love to spend the day with you both, there's some urgent work I need to take care of." There's a new client I'm working with and even though the day out shopping sounds like my idea of heaven, I need to make sure we land this deal.

"Okay, but tonight, it will be the three of us," Carter promises with a mischievous look in his sapphire gaze. An illicit promise.

TWENTY TWO

BENNETT

Leaving Ella last night was difficult, but I needed a moment to process. Everything happened so fast. She was perfect. Taking both of us like she was made to do it. We healed her. I felt it in her touch, heard it in her whispers.

But this morning's meeting was important. I need to keep her safe and I'll do anything in order to ensure her life is no longer threatened by that arsehole. As soon as I walked into the office, I knew something was wrong. Both men I hired left an hour ago, and now I find myself at the place I never wanted to visit again.

"Hello, Dad."

"Bennett, come inside. We need to talk." He glances at me. It's been four years since he's seen my face, but the whisky on his desk tells me nothing's changed. An alcoholic father and a mother who ran off with some drug addict. It's a wonder I actually made something of my life.

"We do need to talk," I tell him, stalking farther into the dimly lit room.

My father has money. A lot of it. But I never took a penny from him. I didn't want his filthy blood money. Nothing he's ever done has been above board. All the deals he made, every pound he earned was nothing but payoffs from criminals. And now, he's got me on his arse for one particular man.

"Do you know this man?" I chuck the photo on his desk, right under his nose. His dark eyes drop to the color photograph, then up at me. Guilt is written all over his wrinkled face. "How can you sit there calmly knowing this arsehole is on the loose?"

"What's got you in such a huff about him? He has nothing to do with you." His eyes meet mine with an expression of anger.

I shake my head at the uncaring façade that he portrays. A man who's been known to prey on innocent girls and my father is in bed with him, so to speak.

"Do you know what he's wanted for?" I don't tell him about Ella. I can't. "This arsehole is going to die and I'll make sure of it." My tone is acidic, but when he stares at me I realize he has no idea what I'm talking about.

"Are you really going to break up a lifelong friendship over a woman?" he finally utters, realizing there's more emotion behind my outburst than I should've let on. He slips into his office chair and watches me, tenting his fingers under his chin.

"Are you fucking kidding me? Carter will be beside me when I drive a fucking knife into this arsehole's chest," I hiss, but he doesn't agree. He waits a beat and continues.

"I sent him away a long time ago. I'm not responsible for what he did when he wasn't here. I'm sure you remember the day he left."

I nod.

"I never denied he did questionable things, which is one of the reasons we sent him to the U.S."

"What the fuck are you talking about?"

"We found out he had a problem," he admits easily.

Yes, I know he has a fucking problem.

"It was after the Hamilton girl came forward."

That's when my world knocks off-kilter. I can't feel the floor beneath my feet. It's as if I've been punched in the gut. Winded. Sick. Bile rises into my throat and it burns.

"Katherine? Carter's sister?"

He nods.

"What the fuck? How did you not report the fucker?" My voice rises and I know everyone on the floor can hear me. However, my father sits calmly like he's just told me about the weather.

Anger.

Rage.

Fury.

My body vibrates with each one of those emotions until I only see red. The monster will pay. I'll fucking ensure he never sees the light of day again.

He meets my gaze and then I see it. The truth of what he did is evident.

"It's your fault, isn't it? She's here because of you," I accuse him because I know it's true. How else would Ella have found me or Carter? It was a sick plan from the start and we played right into it. How the fuck can my father live with knowing what was done to these girls? Katherine has been through the same thing Ella's experienced all because of a sick monster.

"I know you're angry, but you don't understand my thinking. I felt bringing such publicity would hurt our family name as well as the Hamiltons'."

"Like fuck it would! He raped Carter's sister. He's a sick fuck. I'll kill him myself," I growl, pivoting. I pull his door open and glare back at him. "Don't you dare come near me. You're as bad as he is."

With that, I walk out on the man who raised me. The man who taught me who I was. And as I step into the lift, I realize I have no idea who the fuck I am anymore.

"Bennett." My office door flies open and I glance up to find my best friend.

I glance at Ella. She's been taking notes on our new acquisition, but I need to talk to Carter privately. "I'm sorry to cut this short, sweetheart, but I need to speak to Cart about something. I need his help and it can't wait." My body is still fueled with anger as he steps into the office and shuts the door.

"What's up?" The concern on my best friend's face is clear.

When he reaches Ella, he grips her shoulders, rubbing them methodically, which seems to calm all three of us. The tension is mounted high in my office. The three of us shared something intimate and to have them both here relaxes the anger waging war inside me.

"You know I'd do anything I can to help." It's true. He would.

"Ella, I'll call you in once I've spoken to Carter." I'd rather not have Ella here for this.

She stares at me for a moment with worry marring her beautiful face. My words may be gentle toward her, but my tone isn't. Then she nods and leaves us to it. The man I trust my life with cocks his head to the side, staring at me in question.

"I found the man." I need to give him more than that, but I'm not sure how he's going to take it. I didn't do so well with the news, but the problem is, this has more to do with Cart than it does me.

Silence falls around us. It's an angry, rage-fueled hush. He slips into the seat Ella just vacated, waiting and watching for more. I didn't want her to hear the horror Katherine faced. I'm sure the talk of this happening would have the memories flooding her mind sending her into another state of panic.

Carter doesn't question me; he doesn't say anything. The silence is deadly.

"I was at my dad's offices today," I inform him. "My team found the arsehole who's hurt Ella, but there's more to it than that." My voice is a deep rumble.

My phone rings. When I glance down, I notice it's Sarge, the man who's going to find the predator and bring him to me for his last rights.

"Sarge," I answer, listening to his response. "Mate, I need a location on the man in the photo I sent through. I'm not sure about the name he's using at the moment, but can you run a facial recognition on him? Real name Carlo Bianchi, but I have a feeling he's been using an alias."

"Yeah, whatever you need. We'll find him," Sarge responds. "What do you want us to do after we've located him?"

"I need two men on him immediately. Don't engage. This is personal and needs to be handled with the utmost care and privacy." Our eyes meet and realization dawns on his face. There's no mistaking it. We'll handle this. "Thanks."

"My uncle?" he questions. His voice is dangerous. There's venom coursing through him. I see it alight in his eyes. It burns like a goddamn beacon in the night.

"There's more."

"How much fucking more?" he growls, anger

dripping from every word. Sighing, I sit back, trying to figure out how the hell I'm meant to tell him that the man who hurt Ella also hurt his sister.

"His first victim," I utter, dragging my stare to my best friend. "It was Kat." There's no verbal reaction, merely a white-knuckle grip on the arms of his chair. There's a deafening silence that hangs between us once more. This is indeed personal. "My fucking father was in on it. I don't know the details, Cart, but there's some shit that went down. I'll find out what. But we need to keep Ella safe because I have a feeling he's coming for her with revenge in mind."

"I'll take Ella home." He pushes up, stalking to the door. He opens it and steps outside with me hot on his heels. Ella's gaze meets ours as we close the distance between my office and her desk. "I want you home. I'll take you. Stay there until Bennett and I can sort out this mess," he murmurs with pure rage in his tone.

She glances at the paperwork on her desk and responds, "But, I'll—"

"This isn't up for debate." I stare at her.

She knows better than to argue with either of us because her safety is important. I don't want her in public alone. Her tormentor is out there, and we've just confirmed that Carter's uncle is the one who's responsible. We can't tell her. She'll lose it. Once this has been sorted out, I'll make sure she knows we did it for her. Hopefully she'll never have to learn about Carter's uncle being the man who violated and broke her.

"Fine, I'll take my laptop home to work from there."

It's settled. This will end today. He will pay, and I'm going to love every fucking minute.

TWENTY THREE

ELLA

I CAN'T ARGUE WITH TWO ALPHA MEN. IT'S POINTLESS. I push up from the chair and turn to head to my desk. Carter and Bennett haven't told me what they're going to do, but I have a feeling it's not legal.

Shutting down my laptop, I slide it into the black leather satchel along with the charger. I don't need anything else, and when I glance up I find Carter staring at me. "What?"

"You're beautiful. I look at you and wonder what you're doing with us."

I giggle because that's the stupidest thing I've ever heard. Both he and Bennett are handsome. They could be male models. Chiseled, tanned skin under the immaculate suits. Eyes that shine like an expensive pair of gemstones. Every inch of them is perfect.

"Carter, there are times you say the stupidest

things." My retort earns me a smirk and he narrows his eyes at me.

"Ella, you do realize your cheeky mouth is going to earn you a good hard fucking in the backseat of my car," he murmurs hungrily against my cheek.

I don't doubt he's serious about it, and I can't stifle my gasp.

"You say that like it's a punishment," I tease playfully and he steps back, regarding me with a predatory glance. The heat from it has my core pulsing with need. As much as my body protests from both men worshiping me, I still want more.

These men have turned on an insatiable need inside me and all I want is for them to devour me. "Let's go, Princess."

Bennett meets us in the foyer and gives me a hug. "Be careful," he whispers with a soft kiss on my cheek, then leaves us. His hands roam my body, cupping my ass, squeezing hard, causing me to whimper. "I'll be at your apartment soon, sweetheart."

"How are you feeling?" Carter questions me with wariness lacing his tone.

He can't really be jealous, can he? I fix him with a stare and find him curiously studying me.

"I'm feeling good. Happy." My response is short, but I'm sure he can see the emotion on my face.

As we step into the empty elevator, he turns to me. Cupping my face in his hands, he peers at me under those beautiful hooded eyes. "Bennett and I will be doing something… we'll be sorting out a mess." His confession stills us both for a second.

"And you don't want me to be alone. Or anywhere near the office?"

"Bennett's men found something and we're waiting for a location on the man who's been harassing you," he tells me then.

I tense. My heart slams against my chest, leaping into my throat.

"We'll find him. I don't want you to worry."

"I'm not worried. I've chosen two men I know will keep me safe."

He nods as if he's satisfied with my answer and then crashes his mouth down on mine. All the tension that wound him up releases as his tongue sweeps alongside mine in a searing kiss I know will leave me breathless.

When he finally pulls away, the elevator dings and the doors open. I follow him to the car on shaky legs. Every time he kisses me, touches me, or fucks me, I'm a ball of need. I know he's taking me home to keep me safe, but what worries me is what he and Bennett plan to do. I know it has something to do with my stepfather.

Why aren't they telling me more?

As we weave through traffic, Carter reaches for my hand, lacing his fingers through mine. It's a romantic gesture, something that surprises me. It's not that he's not romantic, but the feelings we've found with each other are still so new. I love the feel of his hand in mine. It's like mine was meant to fit into his. Like a key fitting into a lock. He and Bennett have broken down my walls, unlocking the part of me I'd hidden for so long. "A penny for those thoughts, Princess?"

"I'm just thinking about you and Bennett," I answer honestly.

"Are we naked?" he quips on a sinful smirk.

I snap my eyes to his and find amusement dancing on his features, making him look younger than he really is.

"No, you're fully dressed. Stop being an ass."

That earns me a deep chuckle. "An arse?" Another quirk of those full lips that have me squeezing my thighs together.

How can he make me wet with a grin?

"Yes, an overly confident ass actually," I retort playfully.

"Oh, darling, how I'd love your sexy arse in front of me with that little skirt over your hips while you show me that tiny white thong you're wearing."

My mouth drops open as I stare at him in shock. *How the fuck?*

"Don't look so shocked, baby. I know the outline of your body like I know the back of my hand. I can see you're wearing a thong because the smooth material of your skirt hugs those curves I'm tempted to taste right now."

My mouth is still gaped in shock, but the man is as serious as if he's telling me a business deal has just gone wrong. There's no humor in his eyes and when he turns to me, he offers a sly wink and gets out of the car. We've pulled up to my apartment building and I didn't even notice.

The car door is opened for me and Carter offers his hand, which I gratefully accept. Making our way into the building, I lean in and whisper, "It's a shame you have to go out now. After your little alpha male display in the car, I'm rather wet for you," I murmur in his ear, and I hear a deep growl rumbling in his chest.

As soon as we step into the elevator, even before the doors close I find myself against the wall with a hard body pressed against mine. Lifting my leg to hook around his waist, his deft fingers lift my skirt and find the soaked lace of my white panties.

"Mmm, I do love how wet you get for me." His fingers shift the material and dip into my pussy, flicking my clit.

My body tenses, and I roll my hips against his hand.

"Fuck my hand, Ella. Take my fingers in your sweet, little cunt." His filthy words spear me, racing through my blood only to send pleasure to every nerve in my body.

"Carter," I moan when he crooks his fingers inside me, sending me spiraling all before we've even reached the seventh floor. He slips both digits from me and traces my lips with the slick arousal coating both digits.

"I want to taste you on your lips." His tongue darts out, licking the seam of my mouth, sucking my bottom lip in between his teeth as he bites down, turning my core into molten liquid.

Our moment is broken when the doors slide open

and we're deposited in the hallway. I follow Carter as we head toward my apartment door, which he opens and enters first, making sure there's nobody waiting on the other side.

I toe off my shoes and drop my purse on the sofa, inhaling a deep, calming breath. The stress has taken its toll on me and I feel the tension in my shoulders. After my orgasm in the elevator, I thought I'd be relaxed, but knowing I'm about to be alone sends my nerves into disarray.

"What the fuck is this?" Carter's voice drags my attention to the card he's holding in his hand. It's a sleek silver envelope, which I take in confusion.

"Where did you find it?" He glances at me and I can see the worry on his face. After the incident at the restaurant, he knows it can mean only one thing. My stepfather. We both settle on the sofa and my body shivers in fear. I take the envelope from him and rip it open.

"What does it say?"

I lift my gaze to his for a moment before my body convulses with sobs. Carter rips the card from my grasp and reads it. The air around us changes, ignites with rage, and I see his hand trembling with the emotion that's overtaken his body.

I always know where you are, Snowflake.

He drops to the sofa beside me, pulling me into a hug. The force of his arms around me stills my shaking body and I don't know what else to do, so I cry.

"He's here." My words are ragged, as if there's a blade in my throat, slicing me open with each word. My chest tightens in agony at the message inside that card. The promise. The vow. He's coming for me and he'll hurt me. And this time, I don't think he'll stop. This time, I know he'll kill me.

It's quiet for a long while and my tears dry and my sobs fall silent.

"I'm not going anywhere. I'm right here for you. Talk to me, Ella." His voice is soothing, like a balm over fresh wounds, and I revel in it, trying to allow it to heal me, but I don't think he can anymore.

Carter's phone ringing disturbs the now silent sobs coming from me. "Fuck," he grunts.

The word stabs at me, slicing me wide-open as I glance down at the lit-up screen. My heart thuds loudly in my ears and my body locks in fury, rage, and fear.

I find the strength and pull away from the man I trusted. The man I gave everything to. "Fuck you! Get the hell away from me!" My screeching is loud enough to wake the dead and Carter's gaze is pained.

"Ella? Wait—"

When he releases me, I run into the kitchen, pulling a knife from the drawer, and spin on my heel to face him. The liar. "Get. The. Fuck. Out," I hiss and he holds up his hands in defeat.

"Princess—"

"Shut. The. Fuck. Up. Don't you ever come near me again, you lying fucking bastard!" I screech before he can get the nickname he gave me out. I lunge at him, causing him to flinch. Adrenaline shoots through me in an instant, warming my blood. I manage to slice his arm. It's small, but he rears back once more.

He grips me hard and shoves me against the refrigerator, but I don't relent. I fight him as much as he does me. His gaze locked on mine in resignation. His phone interrupts us again and that's when I've had enough of his goddamn lies. I attack him again, but he doesn't allow it.

Instead, he hisses, "Listen to me, Ella."

"We're done. Get the fuck out. Did you play this game with him?" I shove the card at his chest. My voice is hoarse, shrill, and my throat burns in agony. The fear on his face only infuriates me more and I lift my knee, getting him right in the spot I want him, and he keels over. Shoving him toward the door in his crumpled state, I pull it open and he stumbles into the hallway.

He's gripping his cock as he hisses through clenched teeth. "Ella… Listen to me, please." The ringing, his words, everything becomes too much. It's all too much.

"Leave me the fuck alone. We're done. It's done. Do not come near me again." Slamming the door in his face, I lean back against it and slide down the wood. His banging from the other side is loud and echoes around me, but I don't relent. Tears stream down my face, and the sobs choke me as my heart is gripped in the pain from the truth that so violently fucked my world apart.

One man took not only my innocence, but now he's ripped one of the men I love away and I'm left with nothing. I'm not Carter Hamilton's obsession, I'm his. The monster who stole everything from me. And the realization has my body wracked with sobs. When the banging on my door ceases, that's when my world crashes down around me.

I'm alone.

I'm dead inside.

I'm just a broken, tainted little girl.

I'm just a filthy whore.

TWENTY FOUR

CARTER

MOST OF MY YEARS I'VE SPENT INSIDE DIFFERENT women. Each night I'd fuck them and walk away. It didn't matter if they were married or if they had a boyfriend. I wanted to get my dick wet, so I did. I ploughed through half of my sorority, and then most of my personal assistants.

Even though I wanted a long-term relationship, I've never found anyone worthy of my time.

Until her.

Ella Carmel walked into my life.

Now, she's pushed me away without allowing me to explain who he is, why he was calling me. I don't blame her for being scared. I should've told her. We thought it would be easier if she never knew my uncle was the one behind her pain.

Pulling out my phone, I hit dial on Bennett's number.

"I need your help with Ella. We were fine, and then Charles called. My phone was on the sofa between us and she saw the name and photo of my uncle on the screen. She freaked out, called me a lying bastard, and then pulled a kitchen knife on me," I tell him while stalking to my car. Slipping into the driver's seat, I plug in the hands-free kit and pull out onto the road.

He sighs, then chuckles. Bastard. "She stabbed you?"

"No, flesh wound mostly. We need to fix this, but she won't allow me back into the apartment to explain." My office isn't far from here, so I'll grab what I need from there and make contact with Charles. Perhaps I can find out his location.

"She hasn't called me. I'll try her in a few minutes. I wanted to get this done tonight, but Sarge says he's on the move and they lost his trail. We can, however, head over to his apartment." There's a satisfaction in his tone and I have a feeling what we're about to find is nothing short of horrific.

"So far, she's safe. He was calling me, so it means he wants to make contact. We can search his place first, then you can come here and talk some sense into Ella. I can't lose her, Bennett," I warn.

I pull out my phone, hit dial on his number, and wait. When I reach voicemail, I slam the phone on the desk. This is fucking ridiculous.

Bennett still hasn't sent the address. My body is coiled so tight I'm sure it's about to snap.

TWENTY FIVE

ELLA

AS SOON AS I SLAMMED THE DOOR ON CARTER, I cried. I allowed myself to mourn the lies, the pain, and the slicing agony that seemed to want to consume me. Then I got up, showered, and started packing. The suitcase that sits beside me on the sofa taunts me.

I promised myself I wouldn't go back to New York, that I wouldn't walk backward in life, instead look forward, but this has ripped me to pieces.

Silence settles over the apartment. It's never a good sign. For me, the quiet always reminds me. Reaching for the remote, I turn on the television, hoping the noise will calm me down. I know it won't, it's never helped, but I don't have another choice. My fear of having to come face-to-face with the man who hurt me is something I can never become accustomed to.

Bennett and Carter gave me something I can never repay. They showed me the pleasure I had inside me and I can't even begin to describe how much it hurts to walk away from this new life I thought I've found. But when I saw the image on Carter's phone I knew I'd never escape.

Closing my eyes, I recall the pleasure so intense it felt like I was plugged into an electric chair. Every nerve in my body came alive under their touch. I never thought it was possible for me to feel, or care, or love. Carter broke down every wall I built and he gave me the courage to find the one thing I thought I'd lost. My soul.

Curling up with a cup of tea, I take a long sip. The warmth seeps through my body. I haven't answered Bennett's calls, but he hasn't given up. I ended up turning my phone off just to have some quiet time.

It's been two days of ignoring Carter Hamilton and trust me, that's a difficult feat. There's no doubt Carter would have made up some story about why my tormentor was calling him.

The last name may have been different, but it was indeed him.

Closing my eyes, my mind plays the scene from that night over and over again. The call, the card.

Everything made me sick to my stomach. The thought of him finding me. Shaking my head, I push up from the sofa and head back to my kitchen. Before I can fill the tea kettle the buzzer makes me jump.

It's not my intercom. It's the doorbell. Staring at the door as if it's about to attack me, my body on alert, I step toward the phone and before I can move I hear a voice I never expected.

"Ella, open the door. I know you're in there." Bennett Ainsworth, my boss, is at my door. Fuck. "Ella, I'm not leaving this time, so you better answer this damn door."

Shuffling toward it, I unlock the latch and pull the door open, peering up into forest green eyes I could easily get lost in. And I want to. I want to lose myself in them again just for one more night of no pain.

"Mr. Ainsworth, I'm not—"

"I know. May I come in?"

I nod, stepping aside as he enters. He doesn't speak, but I can feel the tension radiating off him in waves. Shutting the door, I turn to face him.

"I'm not feeling well, and I wish you hadn't come here. There are so many things I need to think about right now. I think you should—"

"I think I should find out why you haven't let Carter in. He's been calling nonstop for the past two days. We planned on heading to your stepfather's apartment tonight. My men are tracking his phone. We want to get him when we can corner him." His words cause my stomach to roll.

"That's more reason for me to leave, Bennett. I can't be here anymore. He found me and I need to keep running." Glancing up, I can see he's not buying it. He knows I've found solace with him and his best friend.

"Ella, cut the shit because I'm not going anywhere until you listen to Carter. It's not my secret to tell. But you have to believe he isn't here to hurt you." Bennett reaches for my hand and I allow him to take mine. He looks at me with such sincerity, causing my self-control to slip, and I need to get it back.

Pulling my hand from his, I turn to face the window. "Bennett, I can't." I cast a glance at him over my shoulder, regarding him. He could have been lovely to work for, a sincere, gentle person, but his best friend is not.

"You've been hurt before, but Carter won't hurt you." He watches me for a long while and all I can do is nod. There was something between me and Carter, but he lied. He's hiding something that I can never live with, never forgive. I can't trust him.

"Bennett, with all due respect, I know he's your friend. Please, I need you to stay out of this."

When my eyes find his, I see the agony in them. He's trying to be supportive, but I'm too fucked up to allow anyone into my life right now. I watch him pull out his phone and hit dial. My body tenses because I think he's calling Carter, but when he speaks I relax.

"Lizzie, can you block out my day? I have something urgent to see to." He hangs up and turns to me. "Now, you and I are going to do something fun. Go and get dressed." Even though it's a command, the smile on his face makes me offer one in return.

"What do you mean? Where are we going?"

He stalks toward me. Grabbing both my hands, he places a kiss on each. "I'm taking you to see the sights. Go on. I won't take no for an answer." After the tears I spilled last night, my eyes are puffy and I'm sure they're bloodshot, but the way Bennett stares at me, I feel like the most beautiful woman in the world.

"You do realize I'm still your employee?"

"I do. There's a lot you don't know about me, Ella, and I hope you'll give me the day to show you I'm here for you. I don't want you to leave Ainsworth International."

"I can't be—"

He cuts me off mid-sentence. "I know. Let's just forget the tension and what happened. Let me take you out and you can take the day to decide if you really want to walk away or if you'll give Cart the chance to explain what and why."

I stare at him. There's nothing stopping me from doing this, from forgetting the fear that's held me for far too long. I nod.

"Okay."

He offers me one of those charming smiles and nods. Flopping onto my sofa, he lifts one ankle, crossing it over his opposite knee. "I'll wait right here." He winks and I shake my head.

Heading into the bedroom, I grab my clothes and step into the bathroom. This will have to be a quick shower. Turning on the taps, I wait for the water to heat up and step under the cascading spray.

Using my orange blossom body wash, I lather up and wash my hair. Ten minutes later I'm toweling myself dry. When I glance in the mirror, my reflection is drastically different. My eyes are no longer puffy and red, and I feel better. Stronger.

I am strong. I am strong. I am strong.

"I'll be another ten minutes," I shout toward the living room.

"Take your time, beautiful." His deep rumble echoes through me.

My phone vibrating on the nightstand pulls my attention out of the thoughts running wild in my mind.

Sliding my finger over the screen, I find a message from the man I'm avoiding.

Carter: *You can't hide from me forever, Princess. I won't stop until you let me explain.*

Reading those words have me on edge because I know he won't stop. Turning to my closet without answering the message, I grab my black jeans and a blue shirt. It's dressy but casual enough.

Striding into the living room, I find Bennett in my kitchen with a mug of coffee. He's staring out the window, but when he hears me, he turns and his gaze alights with a smile.

"You look lovely. Are you ready?"

I can't stop the blush from heating my cheeks. "Thank you. I'm just going to grab my purse and we can go." He finishes his drink and sets the mug in the sink.

"I promise, not one mention of my best friend, but I must tell you, he knows I'm with you."

I shrug, but I know it's not as casual as I want it to come across as.

"Bennett, please. Don't ask. I'll allow Carter one chance to explain, just not right now."

He nods, smiles, then follows me to the front door. When I open it my breath hitches. On the small welcome mat is another snow globe with a note attached. I must have stumbled because Bennett's arms are around me.

"Ella, what's wrong?" He practically walks me back to the sofa and once I'm settled, he stalks to the door and picks up the offending item. I watch him pull the note from around it and his gaze locks on mine after he reads it.

"What... I... What does it say?" My whole body is trembling and I can't stop tears from falling. Pain hits me right in the chest and nausea has me pushing off the sofa and racing to the bathroom.

I fall to my knees and heave.

My body wracks as I wretch and the burn in my throat has tears running down my cheeks. I jump when I feel Bennett's hands on my back. He lifts my hair, holding it back as I puke my guts up. I'm still shaking as he rubs slow circles on my back.

"Shhh, I'm here, love. Just try to breathe." His soothing words calm me, but my heart is trying to fight its way through my chest.

I don't know how much time passed. I lose track of everything, until Bennett settles on the bed beside me. He pulls me into his hold and murmurs in my hair.

"I'm going to see Cart. We're heading out to find Charles. I need you to keep the door locked. And under no circumstances, do not open it."

I nod, but I can't find my voice. My throat hurts from throwing up. He presses a kiss to my forehead and rises. Once I'm alone, I curl up under the comforter, but I know sleep will elude me.

Do you know when you see something that scares you to the point of paralysis, when you feel like your body can't take any more? That crippling feeling, that's what I feel knowing the truth.

The lock of the front door clicks, and I can't

help sighing. I wonder if Bennett allowed Carter in because if he did, I'll never forgive him. I needed time.

"Carter, go away," I call out, hoping he'll respect my wishes not to see him.

I turn over to face the entrance, waiting to see those blue eyes that have made me fall into them time and again. The front door clicks closed once more and I take a deep breath. The bedroom door in turn flies open with brute force, slamming into the wall behind it, and I'm face-to-face with the monster from my nightmares.

He's tall, over six feet, with broad shoulders, and a scowl that tells me he's more than angry. His face is wrinkled, pallid skin hanging over his skull that makes him look like a monster, because he is. Thin lips curl into a vengeful grin.

Those gray eyes pierce me like a blade as he stares at me. It feels as if a knife is being twisted in my gut. "Snowflake, it's so good to see you."

I leap from the bed, but there's nowhere to go. Bile burns my throat at those words. He reaches to the side, and when he turns to me again, I notice he's got a large black bag. Shock settles over me, leaving me paralyzed in fear. He's bigger than I remember. Almost scarier.

"What—" As he stalks forward, I shuffle back, but the wall stops me from moving farther away and I realize this is it. The end. My heart thuds against my ribs painfully. I've been scared all my life, but nothing could've prepared me for seeing the monster again.

"Your little boyfriend thought he could fucking outsmart me?" His chuckle is demented. The sinister sound that haunted me my whole life. "I've missed my fragile little Snowflake. Used to be so sweet and innocent, but we all know you're no longer that. Are you?"

"Please, don't do this. Why are you here? How did you find me?" I find my voice, even though it burns to speak. His filthy gaze trails from my feet slowly up my jean-clad legs and the blue shirt I'm wearing, but it feels as if I'm naked.

"Oh, Snowflake, so many questions." He grins maniacally.

I step back until my legs hit the vanity cabinet.

"You're still so pretty. I like the darker hair. It suits you. And your eyes, they make you even more alluring, more tempting. Since you're no longer pure and white, I suppose it's fitting."

After so many years of running I'm stuck here with him. And somehow, I don't think I'm going to survive it. I can't go through this again, just when I got back my life. He pulls something out from the bag he's holding and when my eyes settle on the object I retch. The bile burns my throat and tears spring to my eyes as I shut them.

"Did you miss this, little one? I find pretty little girls love it as much as you did," he hisses. Filthy hunger hangs on his words and I can't look. I can't face what he's holding.

My body trembles and my stomach heaves with fear. There's nothing coming out, but my body convulses. My hands grip my middle, attempting to hold myself together as I fall apart in front of him.

"Don't be so dramatic. I know you loved feeling it inside that filthy whore cunt." His tone changes, switching to the one I remember from all those years ago. All these years and he still has the power to paralyze me. "It worked out so well, Snowflake, when you chased your boyfriend away. He won't be back for a long while." His tone sends terror through me and I realize he knew I was with Carter. He did it on purpose so I'd tell Carter to leave.

Suddenly, Charles reaches out, gripping my hair

at the nape, dragging me farther into the bedroom. He's strong. Even though he's older, his physical strength is no match for me. Shoving me forward, I fall to my knees, but I reach out to catch my fall, and my wrist twists. Pain shoots through my arm and I cry out loud. Something must have broken because the pain is unbearable. The shirt I was wearing is ripped away and I'm left in my white bra.

He uses brute force to turn me over and throw me onto the bed. My body bounces, but before I have time to move, he works the cable ties to secure my hands to the railing of my headboard. Without moving his body, he rears back and swats me hard across the face.

"Shut up," he growls angrily.

My face slams sideways into the corner of the nightstand and all I see is red. Blood drips from my face. Pain shoots through me, causing me to whimper in agony.

"Please—" The rest of my words are muffled by the cloth he shoves in my mouth.

"Now you'll shut your pretty little mouth and let me get reacquainted with your body."

A frown creases my forehead, but when I take a deep breath through my nose everything goes black.

"Snowflake, I need to talk to you."

I glance at my stepfather and smile. He's been going through something that makes him angry all the time and I wish there was some way I could help him. My mom is passed out after the party. She's really tired after looking after me and all my friends.

"Sure, Daddy, what's wrong?" The chair of my desk is cold and I shiver. His gray eyes settle on my chest and I can't help squirming under his intense stare.

"I think you know what's wrong. What you've been doing all this time."

I frown, regarding him warily. Fear runs through my veins as I watch him step closer to me. There's something menacing about his approach, and when he grips my hair, tugging my head back, I let out a whimper.

Pain courses through me and tears spring to my eyes. He's never hurt me. Why is he doing it now? I didn't mean to make him angry. "I didn't—"

"Yes, you fucking did. Acting like a little whore in front of me. You think I don't notice how you wiggle your tiny little ass? Those perky little tits are always on show. Pointing directly at me." He hisses the words in my face and I wince. Spittle from his mouth dots my cheek and the stale smell of beer and cigars has my stomach rolling.

I try to shake my head, but I can't move. His hold on me is too tight. The tears I was holding back spill when I blink and he leans in, licking my cheeks.

"Mmmm… So delicious. I'm going to taste every part of you. I bet you're as sweet as you look, aren't you, my baby?" His other hand gropes my breast, squeezing and mauling it.

"Please—"

"Shut it! Don't you fucking speak. Do you hear me?" He doesn't wait for my answer. Instead, with one strong hand, he grasps my yellow summer dress and rips it from my body. The tattered material is in shreds, not covering me any longer, but instead leaving me bare to his filthy leer.

He pulls me up and drags me over to my bed. Throwing me down like a little rag doll, I bounce and pray someone will help me. That perhaps my mother will wake up and hear. Maybe she'll be able to distract him or something, anything. But that doesn't happen because he grips my ankles, pulling me to the edge of my bed until I'm bent over.

My blue cotton panties are pulled down and a deep animalistic growl vibrates from his throat. "So perfect."

I hear the belt buckle and terror grips me in its fist, holding me steady so the man I once called daddy can violate me. He reaches in front of me and I shiver with trepidation.

He shoves my panties into my mouth and hisses in my ear. "Don't you make one fucking sound, little Snowflake. You're so pure, so beautiful, and you're easy to break." Suddenly burning pain zaps through me, igniting fiery agony between my legs, but when I scream the sound is muffled with the material in my mouth. He grips my wrists in his large rough hands, engulfing me as he holds them behind my back. I can't fight back. There's nothing I can do. Nobody can save me. I have to endure.

I am strong. I am strong. I am strong.

"You like that, slut? You're no longer pure, but you're still my Snowflake, aren't you?" His hips slam into my ass, pushing me against the edge of my bed. His heavy weight pins me in place as he takes something I held dear. Something I was meant to gift the man I loved one day. Fluid runs down the inside of my thighs and I realize my virginity has been robbed from me when I wasn't ready to give it. Fragments of me slowly morph into tiny pieces of the snowflake he's just crushed and as they fall to the ground I vow I'll survive.

I am strong. I am strong. I am strong.

Without warning he pulls out of me and warmth coats my back and my ass. "So pretty and white against your skin. I've marked you, sweet girl. You're a whore now. Do you understand me? You are mine. My filthy tainted whore." With that, he leaves me in my room. The blood trailing down my thighs stains the carpet below. One day it will be his blood. One day I'll make him feel the pain I'm going through.

Charles. The monster from my nightmares.

TWENTY SIX

CARTER

ONCE WE'D KICKED IN THE DOOR TO THE APARTMENT my blood runs cold. It's empty. The fucker got away and I'm fucking angry. Red blurs my vision. Nothing else matters because he has to pay. I don't care how. All that matters now is that he gets what he deserves.

"Where the fuck is he?" My growl is low, menacing, and I don't even recognize my own voice. There's nothing that can compare to the fear and anxiety racing through me right now.

"We'll find him, Carter. My men tracked his phone here. He must be using a burner." Bennett pulls out his phone and hits dial. Stalking through the empty apartment, I find a suitcase and once I flip it open I heave. Inside are photos of both Katherine and Ella. But not the Ella I know now, the one from all those years ago. The girl who had everything ripped from her. The girl who was ruined by a monster.

My heart tightens in my chest, leaving me breathless. "Bennett." The tension radiating through my body is like a coil, tightening so much I'm sure when I snap I'm going to hurt everyone and everything in my path.

"Fuck." He hisses the word and turns on his heel, talking to someone on the phone. I need to get back to my woman. She needs me. Until we can find this fucker I'll spend every fucking second of my time by her side.

When my best friend joins me in the bedroom again I notice the dark expression on his face. When I first met Bennett, he was a kid who was constantly stoned and fucked anything with tits. He's changed a lot over the years, but the one thing I won't forget is what he looks like when he's got murder on the brain.

You see, my best friend almost killed someone once. We were out clubbing one night when we stumbled by a couple having a go at each other. The woman was crying and the man had just laid into her. Bennett walked up to the guy and punched him square in the jaw, knocking him out. Although, he didn't stop there. He straddled the twat and kept punching him. His fists were bloodied when I finally pulled him off.

That night was the first and only night I saw him lose control. It was the only time I've ever been afraid of the man who was like a brother to me. And now, when I see him, I recognize the danger and rage in those green eyes. It's as if someone else has taken over his body.

"I'm going to find that fucking piece of shit and when I do, he'll never be able to walk again. That I promise you." His voice drips with venom and as it coils around me, I feel the warmth, and I know he'll do anything to keep Ella and Kat safe. And I'll never be able to thank him for loving her as much as I do.

Bennett helped me free Ella by giving her something she didn't know she could feel.

Pleasure. Love. Affection.

"We need to get back to her." I cut a glance at him and he nods. He's not listening to me. Well, he is, but his mind is elsewhere. That faraway look in his eyes is evidence that this is affecting him more than he's letting on. "Bennett."

He looks toward me.

"We'll find him."

"I know. I'm just…. fuck… I don't know. I feel like I failed you, like I failed her." That's something we have in common. I've had this instilled into me since I was a child. When you do something, do it with pride. Give your all and now that we've lost Charles, I feel that failure too.

"You haven't failed either of us, mate. We'll find him. Don't doubt." We head to the car and once we're inside I pull my phone from my pocket and type out a message to the woman who's found herself engraved in my heart. Letting her know I'm on my way.

"I should tell you something," Bennett utters then, his voice tentative, and my chest tightens.

"What?" As soon as the question leaves my lips my best friend places a hand on my shoulder. Turning, my eyes meet his. I have a bad feeling he's about to deliver a resounding punch to my gut.

"He knows where she lives. When I was there she received a 'gift'." He lifts his fingers, creating air quotes around the word as he spits it like venom.

Pulling out my phone, I dial her number again. It feels like the millionth time I'm calling. Each ring drags me into the depths of hell. Fear forms a lump in my throat, and my chest aches painfully.

As soon as I hear her voicemail every nerve in my body alights with agony. He's got her. He must have. "We need to get back to Ella, right the fuck now."

He pumps the accelerator until we're tearing through the ground toward the exit.

My best friend knows how to drive like a fucking maniac, and I'm glad he's with me. I would've probably killed myself trying to get to her apartment, because the only thing I see now is red. Blood. Flowing from that evil fucker's body. My hands coated in it because I'll make sure he doesn't survive.

"We'll get her, Carter. I won't tell you to calm down, but just know I'll help you. There's nothing I won't do for you." He glances at me, and when his eyes turn forward, he whispers, "For her."

Casting a glance at him, I realize his feelings for her are deeper than I thought. Even though we'd spoken about our pact, we didn't seal the deal, but this has made it clear. "I know you love her."

He doesn't respond because it's not a question. We pull up to the sidewalk and we both jump from the car before it has time to stop. Making our way inside the building, I find the security guard sitting at his post reading The Evening Standard. Reading a fucking newspaper.

"Has anyone gone up to Ms. Carmel's apartment?"

Dragging his eyes from the article to me, he shakes his head.

"None that I've seen. I've been here all day," he responds calmly. But then again, there is a back entrance which is part of the fire escape. If he'd taken his eye off the camera for even a couple of minutes, he wouldn't have seen someone come and go. Knowing that Bennett's dad is in on this only makes me angrier. He'd have access to this whole building with a snap of his fingers.

Heading to the lift, I push the button for the car. Every second that ticks by has my body aching, thrumming with vengeance and revenge. My blood is hot, boiling like heated lava ready to erupt.

"That fucker needs to die. If he set one hand on her," I hiss at Bennett, who's vibrating with emotion beside me. As the doors slide open, I'm already inside pushing the button for the seventh floor when Bennett steps inside.

The car inches up and so does my blood pressure. I can't deal with this. I'm like a grenade. Ready to blow. And I'm going to blow so hard all over that sick fuck he's not going to know what hit him. But killing him is going to be too fast for him. He needs to suffer.

Bennett's voice rips me from me daydream of blood. "Meet us here. We need your special services."

"Who was that?" I question as he hangs up and we step into the hallway.

"A friend. He knows how to clean up a mess."

I've always known my best friend had a few nasty acquaintances, but now I know it's true. The door to her apartment is closed, and there are no sounds coming from it. I knock twice and wait.

Nothing.

Not a fucking sound.

"Step back," Bennett utters in a tone that tells me I better move or I'll be on my way out as well. He lifts his leg and kicks the door in without breaking a sweat. The living room is empty but what has my senses heightened is her phone lying on the floor near the sofa. The water glass that's shattered on the floor and the sound of nothingness.

No whimpering, no crying, just nothing.

Rushing into the bedroom I find it empty.

She's just fucking gone. Adrenalin kicks in, racing through me like a drug, coursing through my veins, alighting it with fierce urgency.

"Yeah, they're not here. Can you track it?" He's quiet for a little while, then responds again. "Good. Send me the location immediately. Can you get there?"

Walking through the apartment, her scent is everywhere. That soft, orange blossom perfume she loves. That I love. I do love her. My heart is full and it's because of her.

Nothing in my life has ever mattered enough. It's been an ongoing chore to feel anything. But when she walked into my life, into my mind, she stepped into my heart as well.

"We found her."

Glaring at my best friend, he offers a smirk. It's not a cheeky one. It's one filled with revenge and satisfaction.

"Then what the fuck are we waiting for?" Grabbing her phone, I pull the door shut, well, as much of it that will shut. We head to the stairwell and race down to the ground floor. Thank fuck for my cardio every day.

TWENTY SEVEN

ELLA

COLD. I FEEL ICY COLD. IT HURTS TO OPEN MY EYES, but I try anyway. It's really dark. I'm naked, that much is clear, but it's the familiar ache between my legs that shoots fear through me. *Did he hurt me?* I suppose there's nothing I could do to stop him, because as soon as my eyes open, I realize why my muscles are aching.

He's got me attached to a spreader bar. My wrists are cuffed along with my ankles to one black metal bar that has my ass and pussy offered to him like an offering. A sacrifice to the Devil himself.

I'm no longer afraid. I've endured pain before. I was strong enough to escape him once. I'll do it again. Somehow, I'll find a way to get out of this and I'll make sure he feels pain. Not just any pain, but I want to watch him bleed.

I don't know how much time has passed, but

Carter hasn't found me yet.

It's too dark to see anything and I have no way of telling where I actually am.

"My Snowflake is awake. You look beautiful like that. Only your best features are visible." A voice that sends ice running through my veins comes from somewhere behind me.

"Why are you doing this? Why hurt me again?"

A dark chuckle is the only response I get. I didn't think he'd be able to explain why he's such a sick fuck, but I won't stop until he lets me go or kills me. I feel the heat of him behind me. The rough, calloused fingertip that runs down my spine has me shuddering in revulsion that once again I'm at this man's mercy.

"You know why. Because you're my whore."

A shiver of anticipation wracks my body. I know the pain that's about to befall me. *Can I survive this? Will Carter and Bennett find me? Where am I?* There are too many questions running through my mind.

I hear clinking of metal and panic sends a shiver through my body. The ache in my legs and arms has me biting down on my bottom lip until I taste the warm metallic flavor of blood. My stomach rolls as I heave, but nothing comes out.

"Stop acting like a fucking child. You're grown up now. You have a man who fucks you, surely. Or are there two of them, whore? I told you all those years ago, Snowflake, you're mine. Always will be."

Suddenly pain prickles my skin, like tiny needles being pushed into my back, along my spine. I don't know what it is, but something tells me this is going to hurt worse than I remember.

Slowly heat trickles down my spine and I feel numb. Like he's shot something into my blood stream because now I can't feel hot or cold or pain.

"Now to test this sweet little hole I've missed so much."

Without another word, I'm filled. Ripped open. Torn in half. Whatever you want to call it, that's how I feel. Still there's numbness throughout my body, but I know he's penetrated me. I can't say for sure with what. My head is spinning at a million miles a second.

"Please."

"You can keep begging. You can scream. Fuck, I'd love it if you scream. I love hearing those little whimpers. They make my fucking dick hard." A swat on my ass splinters over my skin and the feeling comes back with a vengeance. Heat trickles over my spine nearing my ass. I tense, but it's no use. I'm tied up so tight that any movement is halted by the metal cuffs around my ankles and wrists.

"Feel that, little one. Do you remember when you had me spill my coffee over my shirt?"

The question has my mind racing through memories of when I was a child. A teenager eager to please him. And I remember vividly what happened that night. I was sixteen. It was after he'd first assaulted me.

I'd come home late from school. He was in the kitchen. When he spun around not realizing I was there, we slammed into each other by accident and I knocked the cup of coffee he'd been holding. The whole mug splattered across his shirt and my face.

He was so angry, he'd taken it out on me that night. He was particularly rough. His big, rough hand choked me while his cock was forced inside my dry body. He was unrelenting. I was about to reach the point of suffocation when he let me go, letting me breathe in much needed air.

He laughed. Told me I was a *good girl* for taking it.

"Tell me you fucking remember." The words he spews has spittle flying onto my back, then more heat. The scent of a candle filters through the air and I realize it's hot wax.

As soon as I calm myself from the realization, pain jolts me back to the alert scared little girl as he pours the hot wax over my puckered hole. The sensitive area burns and tears form in my eyes.

"Fucking little whore. You loved it, didn't you? Did you think you can run from me?" The wax cools on my skin, leaving it tight and puckered. His fingers work my tight ring of muscle and I can't stop myself from tensing. I've only ever been with Bennett and Carter. No other man has ever been in there, except for Charles taking what was never his to have.

I've never trusted anyone to come near me. This man had ruined me until the two men I love saved me. My avenging dark angels. Closing my eyes, I picture them. Those devilish smirks, gentle and commanding touches. Love. Affection.

I love them. I didn't think I was capable of that emotion. My past hasn't afforded me the luxury most women have. To trust a man. To really feel a man. But they've given me that and so much more.

They healed me.

They made me whole.

Both men helped me see myself as a woman. And now, as I sit here chained, I realize that for the first time in my life, I'm in love. Not with one man, but with both.

There's nothing that can prepare you for when your life is about to end. As I lie here, I wonder why I didn't just end my life years ago. It would've been so easy to let go and allow death to steal me.

But I thought I was strong. I believed it. Even though I broke each time he came near me, I still held onto the fact that I survived each nightmare. When I was a broken, abused teenager, I could have done it. Taken a razor and sliced my wrists. The pretty red blood mixing with my bath water. I imagined it. So many times over those years I wondered why I even endured it.

I was the silly little girl, the one too scared to fight him. The one too scared to scream, shout, or cry. But now that I'm chained up like an animal I realize I got my chance. I should have done something then.

The blindfold is ripped away from my eyes and I stare into the gray eyes of the monster from my nightmares. "Such a pretty little girl," he utters in a low, gravelly tone. The whisky on his breath is harsh to my nostrils, causing my body to convulse. "You have been on my mind for a long time. I watched you. Seen how beautiful you are. And of course, when I told your boss to send you to London, I knew my nephew would find you utterly alluring." A sinister smirk forms on his face, making him scarier than I remember. He planned this.

"What do you mean?"

"You are working for Ainsworth International. It was my divine plan, Snowflake. And I knew my nephew and his best friend would lay claim to your pretty little ass."

Realization dawns on me that I sent Carter away for the wrong reasons. I believed he was trying to hurt me when all the while, he had no idea. I was stupid. Every part of my body hurts. There isn't anything I can do but hang from the chains above my head. My gaze flits around, taking in the large empty room we're in. It's dark, the only light coming from a small window near the ceiling.

It's cold and I can't stop shivering. As if it's seeped into my sinew and bone. I'll never be warm again.

"Did you think you could hide from me? I knew I'd find you fucking my nephew. He's always been known for sticking his dick in anything with tits."

His chuckle is slightly demented, which sets me on edge. He's drunk, angry, and he's going to hurt me.

He takes two steps toward me, till his body is flush with mine. The stench of his breath has my stomach rolling and I taste the acidic bile in my throat.

"Just let me go. You don't have to do this."

"Oh, that's where you're wrong, Snowflake. I need to do this. I'm about to make sure that not even my nephew wants you." His words tighten the ache in my chest and I realize it's my heart breaking, bit by bit. Not having Carter or Bennett in my life would shatter me. In this short time, I felt connected to them on so many levels. Maybe it's because they healed me. Made me realize I'm a beautiful woman.

"There isn't anything you can do that will make him hate me." Fire flares in my gut as rage takes over and I spit the words at him. I'm not giving up so easily. He'll have to kill me before he breaks me.

"Well, I think there is. You see, I've been watching you. Keeping close tabs on your coming and going. And I know for a fact you're ready for me to finally take what's mine."

"What?"

"I know you've been seeing a doctor to get your

injection. However, my little Snowflake, you're no longer protected. You're primed to be taken and given a little…" He pats my stomach, gently. "Bun in the oven. Aren't you?"

His words send me barreling into darkness. I realize he's right. I should have gone this week for my shot. But since the move, I haven't had a moment to find a doctor yet. My arms strain as I fight to pull them free, only hurting myself in the process.

"No. You're wrong." My words are weaker than I wanted them to be, and he knows it.

"Like fuck I am." His hand rises and I feel the sting of the thick gold ring on my cheek. Blood spurts from my mouth.

I am strong. I am strong. I am strong.

I refuse to cry.

I steel myself, hiding inside my mind. My safe place. But it's changed and morphed. It's become something new and different. Something I recognize as emotion. As feeling. I see it for what it is. Love. The love of Bennett and Carter. Their touches, their kisses, their love.

"Look at me, bitch!"

My eyes open, but I'm cold. Closed off. There's nothing there anymore. No feeling or emotion.

I'll never give this man anything again. His hand reaches up and grips my neck, tightening, choking me.

"You'll remember my face until you die. One day, when you're on your death bed, you'll close those pretty eyes and you'll remember my fucking face." His hate fueled words don't hurt me anymore because I know I'm no longer under his control. It's over.

"No, I won't. You know why? Because you're a sick fuck who'll never control me again. I'll never succumb to you, ever again," I spit in his face and I welcome death. I welcome the end because if this is the way I have to go then so be it.

I'm not a whore. I'm not broken. I'm a fucking woman.

His grip tightens and my vision blurs with little white lights. Stars. The sleepiness takes over, but before it can completely drag me from this life he loosens his hold on me. My lungs fill with air and I take long, choking breaths.

He steps away, pulling a small trolley over to where I'm hanging. My vision clears and the tears I refused to shed spill. Implements. Steel glinting in the dim light has me retching.

I am strong. I am strong. I am strong.

"Now we'll play with my toys. My little fuck doll is going to get fixed today, so I can ensure she always remembers me."

He lifts a silver chain with what look like metal pegs on either end. When he turns to me I recognize what he's holding. Clamps.

He leans in, laving his tongue at my bare breasts, biting down on my nipples till I'm yelping in pain. He straightens and clamps each of them between the tiny metal teeth of the clamps and I can't stop the scream that escapes my lips. "Mmm, I love hearing you scream. It makes me so fucking hard. You've always made my cock hard, Snowflake. Especially in your little school uniform. It took all my restraint to wait until you grew some tits."

Another painful bite rips through my body as he clamps my clit. When he steps back he surveys his work with an evil smirk. "Beautiful."

Picking up his next torture device, he turns it on. The buzz of the thick plastic vibrator echoes through the empty room. "I remember watching you in the bath, your smooth soft skin," he informs me and I can't shut it out. "Every night I fucked your bitch of a mother picturing that tight bald little hole."

I'm shaking my head so fast to stop his words from solidifying in my head. Dizziness takes over and I finally break. Tears spill and I allow them to bathe me.

"I recall how pretty your virtue looked on my thick cock when I stole it," he continues. Placing the vibrator on my clit, he turns it on high, sending painful electric shocks through my body, and I realize it's made to hurt me. "Are you getting wet for me, little one?" he questions and shoves the thick plastic inside me so deep I can feel it hit my womb.

"Fuck you!" My anger flares and I don't know where I'm finding my strength, but I do as I bite back my retort. His laugh frightens me when he pulls the device from my raw sex and walks around me. I know what he's about to do and I brace myself for the pain that comes all too soon and blackness surrounds me.

TWENTY EIGHT

CARTER

THE WAREHOUSE IN FRONT OF US LOOMS IN THE darkness and I know he's there. He has to be. This derelict part of Canary Wharf has been abandoned for months. Another SUV pulls up, and two men exit. Bennett's *team* as he likes to call them.

Both men are dressed in black and they're large, broad, and rock fucking solid. My girl is in there and before they can do anything more, I push forward.

"Carter."

Ignoring Bennett, I race inside and find everything in darkness. The moon's dim light filters through a small window, but other than that, we're bathed in murky shadows. I can't see much, but I realize there's nobody here. Frustration boils inside of me and I'm about to punch a wall when I hear whimpering. Soft, sweet, female. Fuck.

A sliver of light shines from behind me and I

realize one of the men must have brought a flashlight with them. The sight before me has me dropping to my knees. My girl. My woman. My love. Hanging from metal chains. Her body is bloody and her head hangs like a limp doll.

My vision blurs. Tears sting my eyes. Rushing forward, I reach for her face and see her flinch. "No." The word is so soft I would have missed it if I wasn't so close to her.

"Baby, it's me. Please, Ella?" I plead with her to open her eyes and when she does I see every emotion I feel inside flit across those gray orbs. He must've taken her contacts out, because for the first time, I see her real eye color and it's as alluring at the amethyst. I've fucking missed her looking at me. Making me feel like a man. Making me whole.

"Carter?" Her eyebrows crease in confusion and I nod. Her face is bloody and there are bruises that have swollen over one eye, which is almost shut. Her long, dark hair is matted and dirty, but it's the rest of her body that's got me more concerned. The two men manage to undo the chains holding her up and her body falls into my grasp, causing a painful cry to fall from her cracked lips.

"Come on, Princess, you're going home with us."

Bennett hands me the blanket and we wrap it around her. She feels so fragile in my arms and I'm so scared I'm hurting her.

"Get the doc to come to my place," I ask my best friend. Before we can leave we hear a car door slamming from outside somewhere. He's back.

Glancing at Bennett, I can see the anger burning like a wild fire in his eyes. "Let them take care of him. They'll hold him until we can come back," he growls. "Let's get her out of here."

We rush to the door and come face-to-face with the man I share blood with. The monster who not only violated my sister but the woman I love.

"What the fuck is going on here?" He's not even afraid that we found him. He has no concern on his face. "You're taking that dirty little whore?" A sinister laugh escapes his lips.

"How about you get out of the fucking way before I kill you, old man?" I spit at him as the two thugs my best friend brought along make their way to him. His eyes fall on them and he shrinks before my eyes. The evil fucker will get what's coming to him.

My girl murmurs and her hands fist my shirt. It's time to go.

"We'll deal with this," one of the men growls as I pass the monster. "Let us know when you need a location," Sarge utters to Bennett and me.

I wish I could finish this now, but Ella comes first. I can't have her in pain while I deal with him.

"We'll be back."

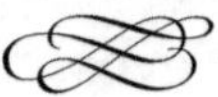

It's been two hours since we arrived at my apartment. The doctor has been and gone. He's given Ella some medication to let her sleep, but the screams she woke up to each time her eyes even fluttered closed have my body alert.

"She's strong. Don't worry so much."

I drag my eyes up to meet those of my best friend. I nod. It's all I can do. Not being there for her bothers me. I should have stayed with her, at her side. Both our phones beep and when I swipe the screen on mine I find a message with a photo attached.

Charles is hanging by those same metal chains. His body is bloody and bruised. I wanted to go there and do it myself, but Bennett said we needed to be here. I agreed. I couldn't leave her, not right now. They've gotten orders to keep him alive as long as possible. From the looks of it, though, he's bleeding out.

I want to hear him take his final breath. I wanted to say things to him that have been on my tongue for days, but as I stare at the image on my phone, I know he's getting what he deserves and so am I. Ella and Bennett are here. We're all three together and nothing will rip us apart this time. I'll make sure of it.

Taking a deep breath, I let it out and sit back. "It's over." Relief washes over me then. Knowing one less predator is out there makes me feel better. The fact he was related to me makes me sick to my stomach.

"Carter, you need to get out of your head," Bennett tells me, settling on the sofa beside me. It's been a long while since we've really talked. Our emotions have been all over the place, but when I look at him, I realize we'll all be together soon enough.

"Once Ella has healed, I want us to propose. Both of us. We can either each get her a ring or some token. She's not alone anymore and neither are we," I tell him. Taking in my best friend, I can't help smiling. He nods in agreement.

"What do you think she'll want us to do?" I ask

him.

His brow creases in confusion as he regards me. I made my decision the moment I saw how he fought to find her. To save the woman we love.

"Do you think she'll be able to give this a chance?"

My best friend stares at me for a moment before taking my hand in his. "We will have her. She's ours. Ever since she walked into my office I knew. The thing is, I never expected to love her so much. It's consuming."

"It is." Our pact was always in the back of my mind, but when Bennett leans in, his lips crash onto mine. The heat of him, his tongue fighting for dominance, which I don't relinquish. I never thought of myself as bisexual. Not at all, but with him, I feel it down to my bones. We've tried to keep our friendship platonic, but there are moments we slip. Like right now as he pushes me onto the sofa. His body looms over mine.

"I love her. I love you. It makes sense," he tells me. His hand is on the bulge in my trousers. My cock agrees. It wants them both. I know Ella doesn't just love me, she loves him too. I'm not going to allow her to lose stability, when she needs it now more than ever.

I grasp his face in my hands, pulling him closer. I need this. I want her and I want him. I lean up to kiss him. Our tongues duel. His erection presses into my thigh and mine throbs in his hold.

"Are you sure?" His smile is wide and I know there's no stopping this. There's love that simmers through the three of us and it won't stop now, and I hope it never stops.

"We do this and there's no turning back. You hurt her—"

"I know. There's no chance I'll ever hurt her or you. If she chooses us both, then I'll give her everything. She'll smile every day. I love her, Carter." His promise cements what I wanted to hear, what I already knew.

"She's our priority now," I utter. My body is alight with need. I want to be with them right now. I'm hungry for intimacy.

"There's nothing that will take away those feelings, mate. We've finally found our girl and all I want to do is fuck you both until you're screaming my name," Bennett mumbles quietly. His voice is laced with need and desire I feel to my bones. Silence falls between us and for the first time in a long while I'm not sure what to say to him. My mind wanders to the first time I met Bennett.

"Who are you?" I question the new boy. I'm sitting in detention and Mr. Douche who's supposed to be watching us fucked off. Leaving five seventeen-year-olds alone in a classroom is not going to bode well for him.

"Ainsworth," he grumbles.

I can tell he wants to come off as a hard arse, but he's not. His eyes are a deep green, which reminds me of the fresh new leaves on a tree in spring. Nothing like I've ever seen before. Bright and almost see-through.

"What kind of name is that?" I chuckle, but he stares at me deadpan. Fuck, he's going to be fun to be around. He watches me for a moment longer before sliding into the seat beside me.

"Bennett Ainsworth. It's my last name, wanker." He curses in his accent, which sounds like he's from up North. His shirt is wrinkled and his tie is undone. I think we could be great friends.

"Hamilton, Carter Hamilton." I reach out my hand and he stares at it like I've got the fucking plague. Another beat, but I don't move. In the end, he grips my hand in a firm shake.

"So, we're friends now, Cart?" he questions, shortening my name like we've known each other for years. No other

person ever calls me that, they know better, but for some reason, I allow Bennett to use that nickname.

Shrugging, I respond, "Yeah, I guess so."

The bell rings at that moment and we shoot up from the small desks. We head down the steps, with my new friend beside me. I stop suddenly, remembering I need to get my sister.

"What the fuck?" He glares at me.

"I need to get Kat." I motion toward the sports field. She had her piano practice after school and I can see all the girls huddled outside the classroom.

"Who's Kat? Your girl?"

"No, my sister." As we reach the girls, Katherine runs up to us. Her curly brown hair bops behind her and her amber eyes shine with mischief. She's a handful and I have to keep her in line. If I don't, I'm sure my sister will get herself into so much shit.

"Hi, I'm Kat." She offers her hand to Bennett and he chuckles and I'm sure I see her blush.

Oh, fuck no!

"Yeah, this is Bennett. Let's go," I grumble in response to her flirting. I tug her along and we head out to the parking lot. I turn to him and take in the look he gives my sister. This is going to be a fucking pain in the arse. "Do you need a lift?" I ask.

He nods. "Aye, that will be good. Thanks."

I watch my sister flop onto the backseat before I tug him by the collar. "Don't you lay a fucking hand on her or I'll cut your balls off and feed them to you while the whole school watches. Do you understand me?" I growl under my breath, but all it earns me is a chuckle.

"Yeah, yeah. We'll see."

When I open my mouth the words just come to me. "I think I loved you since the moment I met you in detention. I may have hidden those feelings for a long time, but they were there. Now, we've got the perfect life. The perfect girl. And I have you. Ultimately, though, it is her choice."

His gaze snaps to mine with affection in it and I know it's something he's thought of all the times we've been together. "You sure you want the world to know you're into dick and pussy?" he questions with a chuckle, watching me for any uncertainty.

I nod. "I do." This is something I want to do for her, for me, and for him.

Hopefully over time we can erase Ella's pain. There's nothing I wouldn't do for her.

There's love between us.

A triad of hearts, love, and devotion.

"Then so be it," he confirms, his mouth on mine once more in a tender, commanding kiss and I groan into his mouth, savoring the taste of my best friend.

TWENTY NINE

ELLA

*I*T'S SO DARK. WHY IS IT SO DARK? MY EYES CRACK OPEN AND *I find myself in a cold, dank room. The walls are a sickly gray color that reminds me of a cellar. Or a prison. Pushing up, I find the door to the tiny room closed. It's steel with a big lock in place. Swinging my feet over the edge of the bed, I race to the entrance and bang on the door. "Hello! Is anyone there? Carter?" My voice is strangled with fear and I can't stop my heart racing.*

It's dark, but I can make out the faint light of the moon. No answer comes from my screaming. I'm alone. No one's here to save me. Did he find me? Will Carter save me this time? Somehow, I doubt it.

My body trembles in the cold room. I'm dressed in the tiny panties I put on after my shower earlier. The vest top is made of thin cotton that doesn't protect me from the elements. I glance up at the tiny square close to the celling. The only reason I can make it out is because the stars are out, but they're not enough to light my prison.

I strain my ears again, but I don't hear anything from the other side of the thick metal door. Running my hands over the walls, I try to find some chink in the armor that surrounds me, holding me in.

It feels like hours later. I can't even feel my fingers, so I curl up on the cot I woke up on and try to warm myself. I've never been so cold. So afraid. As my eyes flutter closed, I hear it. The sound of a lock clicking and suddenly the door is shoved open.

"There's my little snowflake." He's here.

I've run and run, but he's finally caught up with me and I have a feeling this time I'm not going to escape. He stalks toward me, bigger, bolder, and stronger. He reaches out and grips my hair, pulling me from my sanctuary on the bed, and holds me up, making me kneel on the floor. The roots of my hair burn as he tugs me around like a limp doll.

"Why?" I peer up at him, but my question goes unheeded. My body trembles as fear washes over me. As if a poison is slowly running through my veins, I feel myself surrender. Fighting for so many years is finally catching up to me. I can't be strong forever. I can't allow myself to defend the inevitable.

"This time you won't leave me. There's no running.

I've made sacrifices to be with you, Snowflake, and this time you won't run to him. He's done. I've made sure my nephew will never bother us again." He pulls me up by my neck, tightening his grasp.

I reach up and grip his wrist, clawing at it, trying to find air, but there's none. No reprieve and the darkness steals me.

"Ella."

A beeping noise drags me from a deep sleep. When my eyes crack open I find blue eyes staring back at me and the hospital room I'm in is blindingly white. "There's my Princess." His smile is angelic. Beautiful. Perfect.

"Am I dead?" My head is foggy and I'm sure I'm either dead or drugged.

"They don't make angels like me in heaven, baby." His cheeky wink has me giggling. Pain shoots through every inch of my body and I wince. "Are you hungry? I have some lunch ready for you, unless you just want some coffee? Or I can get you juice." His eagerness is endearing, slowly sinking into my heart and filling it with love.

"Carter, just you. I just need you."

His hand finds mine and the heat of his skin on

mine calms me. It's only then I realize I'm in a very fancy hospital room. "Why am I here?"

"Because you're not fucking leaving my side again. Ever. After you get out of here, you're going home with me." The serious tone makes me smile. I don't want to leave him again. I feel safer here than anywhere else, and I need to apologize to him. I sent him away, believing he was working with his uncle when all the while he was trying to keep me safe.

"I won't. I promise."

"Look, Ella, I know you've just woken up, but we need to talk." His voice is serious and I know there's so much we need to say to each other.

I nod, my eyes never leaving his. Realizing I've fallen for him and his best friend is something I need to come to terms with. After what happened I can't lose them. Both men have given me strength before, and I hope they'll do it again. I want to be independent, but I want to be theirs. They offered it to me once before, and it's time I accept this. Loving two men. Wanting two men.

It's my choice.

First, though, it's time I go for therapy. It's time I drag my life back on track.

"I know, but can you kiss me first?" I don't know

where the question comes from, but the smile I'm awarded with is magical. His face lights up and those blue eyes glow with happiness.

"You don't have to ask me twice." He growls. Leaning in, his lips find mine and I savor the taste of coffee and Carter. His flavor intoxicates me, thrumming through my veins, heating my blood. When his tongue swipes along my lips, I part them for him, allowing him inside the one part of my body that doesn't hurt.

Our tongues dance in a sensual rhythm. I savor it for a moment longer before placing my hands on his chest. I push until he breaks the kiss.

"Did I hurt you?" His frown is adorable and I know he's worried about me.

Shaking my head, I turn my gaze to the large windows from my hospital room that overlook the city. From the bed, I can see the spires and rooftops of London sprawled below.

"No, I just… I mean, I need to tell you something." My heart thuds in my chest. Yes, I'm nervous. I feel like a fucking teenager, but I'm not. I'm an adult and I'm allowed to feel this. To say this.

"You know you can tell me anything, right?" he murmurs.

I nod. I wanted to say it at the perfect moment. A time when I'm not in pain and aching, but there's never a perfect moment. I've learned that life is there. If you don't grasp it, then you'll never move forward and that's what I need to do now.

"Is Bennett here?" I question and he nods with a smile.

"Ainsworth, get your arse in here," he calls to the doorway which leads off from the room I'm in and there, in his disheveled shirt and trousers, is the other man I love.

"Can you both join me?"

When Bennett settles on the other side of the bed, I'm once more cocooned in love.

"I was in so much pain for so long. You've both been my knights, saving me, healing me. And while Charles had me, I realized something." I flit my gaze between the two men. "I love you," I tell Carter, then cast a glance at Bennett. "I love you," I murmur the words while staring into his eyes.

The air around us sparks like a storm brewing and the desire is thick between us, as it always is. "I love you too, Princess," Carter whispers across my cheek.

"And I love you too, sweetheart," Bennett

growls in my ear. Their words coat me in warmth, in yearning, and the heat of them surrounds me, keeping me safe.

"I want you to stay here. There will be no argument," Carter informs me. His index finger lifts my chin until we're staring at each other. "Do you understand me?" His commanding tone is back and I smile.

"Yes, Carter." His domineering presence makes me feel safe and as much as I'd like to refuse and be in my own apartment I know I'd feel safer here.

"Now, are you hungry?" He pushes up from the bed, his gaze never leaving mine.

"Please. Can I have a coffee as well?"

He nods. Planting a soft kiss on my forehead, he strides from the room in his confident manner. I lean back on the headboard, feeling my eyes flutter closed, and I shuffle into the crook of Bennett's arm. Exhaustion overtakes me, and sleep drags me under.

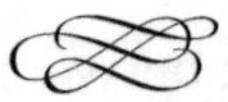

"Ella?" A warm hand on my shoulder pulls me from a dreamless sleep. "Baby, do you want to eat now?" Carter is dressed in only a pair of blue sweatpants and the way his T-shirt molds to his chiseled torso teases me and I can't stop licking my lips. "Oi, eyes up here. I'm not a piece of meat." His teasing tone is light and relaxed, and I have to smile.

"Not my fault you're half naked," I tell him indignantly. Feeling myself blush, I push up to sit against the headboard and grab the mug.

"Princess, behave. You're in pain and I want you to rest, and we need to talk."

Taking a sip of the warm black liquid, I savor the heat that seems to seep into my bones. I was naked for so long that I didn't think I'd ever be warm again. But now, being here with Carter I am. He's always made me feel safe.

A large figure looms in the doorway. Bennett's also dressed in a pair of sweats. Both men look like they've been molded, sculpted by a master artist. The only difference is Bennett's ink that covers his shoulder, pec, and part of his ribs.

"I am behaved," I tell Carter, but my eyes are glued to Bennett as he enters and settles on the bed. "I'm innocently drinking my amazing coffee that one of my amazing boyfriends brought for me." Glancing at him, I find his lips tugging into a sweet smile.

"Boyfriend? Mmm... I don't think I've been called that before, but I'll take it." His grin is priceless, and I hope I get to see it all the time. He places the tray of food on my lap. There's French toast, orange juice, and honey. "I want you to eat okay, Princess?"

I nod, already reaching for the honey and drizzling it over the thick slice of toast.

His groan doesn't go unnoticed and I bite the inside of my cheek to keep from giggling. It was only hours ago that I didn't think I'd make it through the night, or day, but now I'm as safe as I've ever been.

He straightens and walks over to the window, leaving me with his best friend, who's taken to feeding me the delicious food. Bennett's gaze is locked on my lips and he leans in to lick away the sticky syrup.

"Is something wrong, Carter?" I question, noticing Carter's rigid stance.

He shakes his head and turns to me. I realize he's not mentioned what happened to Charles. I wish he'd just tell me, but I don't want to force it. I'm not sure I'm ready to hear the outcome of that monster's life. However, I don't think he's alive anymore. As long as he's dead I don't care how or who did it.

"No, sweetheart. Nothing at all," Bennett responds for Carter.

I nod while I devour my breakfast but keep my eyes on both men. Once I've finished everything on the tray much to Carter and Bennett's satisfaction, I whisper a quiet *thank you*.

"It's a pleasure, Ella. Anything for you, sweet Princess." Carter takes the tray and disappears down the hallway, and I have to glance at Bennett to ask.

"Is everything okay?"

"We do need to talk to you, but Cart thought it would be easier for me to do it. He's nervous."

"Why?" Now I'm utterly confused. I thought we were settled, but something is niggling at both men, which has me curious.

"He's… He and I are…" Bennett's smile is bright, crinkling the corners of his eyes, making him look so much younger than his thirty-six years. "We've been together a few times in the past, and the women we've been with have always enjoyed it. Carter and I want you to know if you're not comfortable—"

"Nothing would turn me on more than to see my two alpha males together. The thought of you both kissing and touching, and…" I trail off. My cheeks heating is the only answer he needs.

"That's what I thought." He winks, pressing a kiss to the top of my head, and I lean into his hold, needing the affection.

Even though sex has hung heavy in the air around us, I'm not ready. And I know both men will wait forever for me.

The psychologist stares at me for a moment. Her glasses are perched on her nose. Her big blue eyes peek over the top of the rims.

"And you haven't been intimate since?"

I've just informed her about what happened. About my childhood and what happened when *he* took me.

"No, I've..." My words taper off. Silence hangs heavy as emotion chokes me. "It's been a while since I've even thought about it."

I feel the tears. They burn the same way the wax had heated my skin to an unbearable level. Strangely, pleasure and pain can come from one object, and when Charles held the candle, he instilled pain so profound, I can't even bear to be near a lit flame.

"That's only normal, Ella. There's nothing wrong

with needing space and time. Some people take years, some months. It depends on your support system and your inner strength."

My eyes meet hers. She seems so sincere with the way she speaks. It's only my fifth session, but I feel as if I can confide in her.

"Last time you were here you said you'd like to speak to your mother. Perhaps we should do that?" she questions.

I nod slowly, still unsure if I want to hear her voice, her explanations for allowing me to live through the nightmares.

"I can call her right now. We don't have to, but…" Her voice is gentle, coaxing me to say yes. "It might ease the heartache."

I nod once more in agreement.

She picks up her phone, tapping at the keys. It's on speaker, loud, jarring. My senses are on overload when I hear her familiar voice.

"Hello," my mother answers.

"Mrs. Carmel," Dr. Hastings says. "I'm a doctor currently treating your daughter, Ella," she offers.

A gasp from the other end of the line tells me she wasn't expecting that.

"EllBell," the voice I've missed for so long utters

as pain laces the name she gave me as a child. "Are you there?"

"Mom," finding my voice, I utter the word I haven't said in years, a long, long time. The emotion choking me is a lump in my throat that's slowly stealing my breath.

"Baby, where are you? Please tell me he didn't find you?" she asks in a ragged voice.

Anger licks its way through me, as if a match has been struck and flames are now dancing in my veins. All these years she knew. There's no other explanation.

"Did you…?" I swallow back the fury. "Did you know what he did to me?" My question hangs in the air, above my head like a weighted balloon. Depending on her answer, I realize I could lose my mother forever. "Answer me!"

"Yes, I… I'm so sorry, baby," she tells me, but I no longer hear her.

The world tilts on its axis, leaving me reeling from her confession. For two long years, I was the victim to a monster and my mother allowed it to happen. She sat back while her daughter was violated in the most disgusting ways and she did nothing.

"You're sorry?" I rise, pacing back and forth. My

body vibrates as if it's alive, electricity sparking through me. A thunderstorm wracks through me like it does to the ocean. The waves crash around me, pulling deeper into the abyss. Darkness.

"Please, EllBell," she tries again, but I can't.

This isn't the woman I grew to love until my sixteenth birthday. I believed she was clueless because I needed her to be. My pain, my agony that ripped me apart for years was something my mother allowed to happen. Why? Was she so desperate for a man in her life?

"I hate you," I tell the phone. The piece of plastic that doesn't mean anything to me feels my wrath, and I hope deep down, my words seep over the line and into her heart. I want to make her pay as much as I wanted him to pay.

"Baby girl." Her words only fuel me further, sending me into a dark rage. I don't move anymore. I'm still. I'm calm. But inside my turmoil burns me.

"I'm not your fucking baby girl," I bite out angrily. "Do you understand me? I'm not your fucking daughter."

I am strong. I am strong. I am strong.

"Ella," Dr. Hastings murmurs. Her hand lands on my shoulder in an attempt to calm me, but fury is the only thing I see. It blurs my vision.

Picking up the phone, I hold it to my ear. "If you ever come near me, ever try to contact me, I'll kill you myself. I want nothing to do with you." I press the end call button, meeting my doctor's worried gaze. "I need another session."

"I know." She nods. "I'm sorry about..." Her words are sad, her tone softer than normal. She walks over to her desk. I watch her press the button for her receptionist. "Please send him in now. We're done," she speaks to the machine. Her gaze lifts to mine. "We'll set another appointment for Friday. It will give you a day to mull over everything and I want to hear your thoughts on everything. From there, we'll move on to healing." Her coldness gives me strength. She's good. I feel comfortable with her.

The door opens and Bennett stalks in. "You okay, sweetheart?" he questions worriedly.

I nod.

"Come here." He opens his arms, waiting for me to take the step. They've each given me this, a choice. He and Carter have been there for me as I heal, as I find my footing again. Without needing to think too much about it, I fall into Bennett's arms. I'm safe here. Warm. Loved.

"That's it for today. You're welcome to take her home."

We make our way out of the office with my face buried in Bennett's white button-up. My heart cracked open wide from my mother's confession. I should've asked her why, but to be honest, I don't want to know. I have nothing more to say to her. My life is here now. With the two men who have come to love me as much as I do them.

THIRTY

CARTER

THE APARTMENT DOOR OPENS, AND BENNETT AND Ella step inside the space. Her face is a picture of pain and agony. I'm on my feet in seconds, wanting to be close to her, to hold her, but her hand flies up before I have time to take a step toward her.

"I need time." Three small words that slam right into my chest. She leaves us staring at her retreating form as she makes her way straight to the bathroom which is just off the bedroom, locking the door and turning on the shower. I feel her sadness down to my bones.

"What the fuck happened?" I turn to my best friend.

Our gazes lock in a standoff. I should've been there, but I needed to meet with my parents and their lawyer. I've proceeded in pressing charges against them both. We're keeping it out of the media, but my father is going away for a very long fucking time.

The fact that he knew what happened to Kat and did nothing only solidified my decision. He was more concerned about marring the Hamilton name. When Bennett's father offered him a way out by sending Charles to America, my father took the easy route and ignored the fact that my uncle is a sick individual.

I know Bennett will want revenge on his father, and perhaps one day we'll be able to get that. But for now, the focus is on my family. Learning that Charles blackmailed both Dad and James Ainsworth, I finally realize that I'm no longer a part of this family. I don't want to be.

As for my mother, she's leaving, heading back to Italy. Charles was her older brother, and it was his fault both of the women in my life had been hurt.

I want nothing to do with my parents. With the Hamilton or the Bianchi name. My uncle had always been Charles to us, but his real name was Carlo Bianchi, and that's why Ella didn't realize I was related to him. Not knowing my mother, she would've never guessed that a sick motherfucker like that was my family.

"What did the coppers say?"

"Dad is being put away. I don't want him near me. He claimed that he was worried about losing the business, but it was James who used his contacts to get Charles out of the country." I inform my best friend about his father's shady dealings.

"I'm going to make sure he pays," Bennett's voice is steel—cold and harsh.

"We will." My gaze meets his. "I have a choice to make," I tell him, settling on the couch.

"What?" Bennett's curious. He knows how much I respected my family. Even though my father pushed me to do shit I didn't want to do, like study business when I wanted to do law, there was always love in my family, or so I thought.

"Do I sell Hamilton International, or do I keep it going?"

My best friend takes my hand, gripping it in his. The emotion in his expression is almost gentle, but there's a seriousness that causes his jaw to tick with frustration.

"Do you want it? I mean, would you like to take it over and run it by yourself?"

His thumb swirls over my palm, calming me. For years we've played, had fun. This is the first time

Bennett's touch is more than just us having fun. This time I realize I've always loved him, more than a friend.

"No," I respond, finding my confidence in what I want to do. When you spend your life being trained to be someone and find out it was all a lie, it's jarring. "I'm going to move on. I've spoken to a lawyer. We can sell the company and I can use the money to start something new. Something without their imprint on it."

Bennett opens his mouth to respond, but the bedroom door flies open, and our princess walks out, looking refreshed, new. Dressed in a white fluffy robe and nothing else. Her hair is wet, hanging down her back.

"Are you okay?" My question causes her to glance at me, then nod. A small smile tugs at her lips. It doesn't look like a happy one, and I'm curious.

"Today," she starts, settling between us as she always does. "I spoke to my mother." Her confession has both Bennett and me staring at her, then at each other. "She knew."

Those two words break her. I see it before me. After everything she endured, all the pain and agony my uncle put her through, she didn't look like this, so… shattered.

"All this time, she allowed it to happen." She swallows, her throat working, her pulse thrumming against the delicate skin of her neck. I want to hold her, but she needs to make the move. "I've been so broken all this time. Each day was like walking through quicksand, trying to stay afloat. My mother," she utters, her gaze flitting between us. "She allowed him to do those things to me." That's when she takes my hand and Bennett's and holds them so tight, I'm sure she's stopping my blood flow.

"Sweetheart," my best friend starts, but she shakes her head, shushing him.

"I'm nowhere near ready for this, but I need it." Her words are raw, ragged, and husky. "I want you both to open my robe," she tells us on a whisper. Placing our hands on the towel material, she leads us to do as she says. The robe falls open and we both suck in a breath. Her form is perfection, her flesh wet and bare. Every inch of her is naked.

"What are you doing, Princess?" I don't recognize my own voice. It's heavy with confusion and desire. Yearning to have her once more, it ignites my love for her. My need to protect her.

"Just let me be." She closes her eyes, taking our hands. We allow her the control. With every gentle caress, she shudders violently as if she's in pain. When she whimpers, I see the tears trickling from her lashes. "He made me believe I was nothing."

She leads my hand to her full, heavy breast, and Bennett's to the other. Our touch must be healing, because the more she cries, the more she tells us. Tears fall heavily from her eyes. The agony that screws up her face makes me want to pull my hand away, but somehow, I know she needs this.

"He took. Every night. Every day." Her lips move with the dark confession. "I was no longer a girl." She doesn't allow us lower than her waist. But her legs are slightly open, just barely. Enough to get a peek of what's between her thighs. "All this time, I walked around convinced I was wrong. But then you both came to me…"

She opens her eyes, looking at me, then Bennett. No more words come. Instead, she rises, dropping our hands. The robe that once covered her falls to the floor. When she turns to face us, standing between us, she watches as our hungry gazes travel over her.

"You heal me every day. And one day, when I can stand it again, I want you to fuck me. But right now, all I need is to take it one step at a time."

"Anything you need," I assure her. I'm hard. I can't stop it. When I look at her, it's something that cannot be helped. She's perfect, beautiful, and she belongs to us.

"You know we're always here for you," Bennett tells her.

She smiles, nods. Then covers herself once more. We watch her walk to the bedroom, and moments later, when we check on her, she's curled in the fetal position on my bed.

"Do you think she'll ever be healed?" he asks.

"Yes. She's strong. She's done it before on her own. This time, she has us."

I watch her clean. She's been slowly allowing us back in. It's been almost a month since her ordeal and I've been watching her like a hawk. She hardly has time alone. Between work and home she has two alpha men following her around. I'm sure she's tired of it, but I'm so scared of losing her.

There's one thing I need to talk to her about. Bennett and I have been looking around for a house. Just outside the city where the three of us can live.

I'm looking forward to seeing her smile when I show her the space.

The garden is big enough for her to potter around in. There's enough rooms for kids, lots of them. And there's a suite where we'll be able to spend time together. Every night.

"Are you going to sit there and stare at me all day, or are you going to come over here and help me?" Her cheekiness is returning, which is a good sign. A strong woman who seems to flourish with the love she receives. And it's doubled up with both men at her beck and call.

"Your cheeky mouth will be punished, Princess."

Pushing up from the sofa, I head into the kitchen and find her on her knees. She's scrubbing out the oven, which is spotless, but I let her do her thing. It's her release. We've gone to counselling together and her therapist suggested she find something to focus on. If she's not working and finding new property for me, she's at home, reading, writing, or cleaning.

"And how on earth do you plan on punishing me, Carter?" Gray eyes peer up at me with amusement. Since we rescued her, I told her I wanted the real her. No more contacts and she's grown out the blond hair she's been born with.

We haven't really been intimate for weeks. Since she asked for time, Bennett and I have given her that. It's killing us both. I can tell he's as frustrated as I am. As much as I am a gentleman, I'm a savage too, and I'd love to unleash it on her cheeky mouth.

The front door opens and my best friend stalks in. He looks utterly stressed.

"Are you okay?"

"Yeah," he mutters, dropping his keys and phone on the counter. "I just had a long meeting with a new client."

"Aww." Ella rises as she coos. Barefoot, she pads over to Bennett and circles her arms around his waist. The tension eases from his shoulders, but I can tell he's stressed.

"Our little Princess was just toying with me," I inform my best friend over her head. "I'm thinking she's enjoying giving us blue balls."

His lips quirk and she spins around, staring at me.

"Maybe I can ease that for you both." Her voice is sultry, that of a lioness about to devour her dinner. Her eyes are hooded as she peeks at me through those long lashes. "Why don't you both go sit down?"

As our girl requested, we head to the sofa and settle in beside each other. Moments later, she joins us, sitting on the opposite seat, watching us intently.

"It's been too long since I've been with you both. It took me time to heal, to feel real again, but there's something that's been on my mind since Bennett mentioned it."

I cast a quick glance his way, then drag my gaze back to her.

"I want to see you both. I mean, I've fantasized about seeing you together, sexually." She's taking control and I let her.

I nod. This is something I knew she'd want and now that it's happening, my cock has hardened in anticipation.

Bennett unbuttons his white shirt, while I undo my black one. We move together, in sync with the other. Her eyes are wide, excited, filled with desire. Bennett leans over toward me, my mouth finding his in a bruising kiss. Our hands are all over the other. I find his bulge, squeezing it through his dark trousers. We groan in unison, two hungry lions with a lioness waiting with bated breath to join us.

Lust courses through my veins when I see her crawl over to us. A sleek hunter, a predator. She's exquisite and I know tonight there will be no holding back because this woman is getting fucked.

"Are you sure about this, Ella?" I question as she reaches us.

She doesn't respond, but instead rakes her nails down each of our bare chests, toward our stomachs. My mind is already spiraling with making her scream while she unravels.

Her slender fingers find the buckle and zipper of my trousers and in no time, I'm naked from the waist down. She moves over to my best friend and does the same, her delicate hands grip our cocks, stroking them slowly, gently, and reverently.

"I want you both so much." Six words that have my cock throbbing. She smiles up at both of us, teasing our dicks, and I'm sure I'm about to come right there. Gray, stormy eyes shimmer with hunger. The yearning of her wanting me sets my body alight.

"I want you too, Princess, but—"

My sentence is halted by her mouth enveloping my cock and taking me deep until the crown nudges the back of her throat. She lifts her head and I slip out of the heat and immediately need it again. Her head bops up and down. It's slow, teasing. There's no rushing her and I don't want to fist her hair like I'm dying to. She's in control and she's got me by the balls. Literally.

Her mouth pops off right before my release shoots up my dick and she takes Bennett in her mouth, pleasuring him with soft gurgling sounds. His mouth is on mine once more and his hand is in my hair, fisting it hard. I'm beyond reason at this point. All I need is to fuck.

Her mouth moves back to my cock, inhaling me. It's the only way to describe it. It's her worshiping my manhood and I'm about to shoot my seed into her throat.

"Princess, I'm so close," I warn her, but she doesn't stop. My balls tighten and I grip the sofa so tight, my knuckles turn white. *Shit. Oh God.* "Princess, your mouth, fuck…"

She swallows me whole, humming, allowing the vibration from her throat to send me over the edge. Ripping me from this world into euphoria. My head drops back as I buck into her mouth. Spurting down her throat, I feel her working to swallow all I have for her.

Fucking shit. My mind is blank, my body locks, and I shudder.

Her tongue traces every inch of my softening erection. Licking, tasting, savoring.

Suddenly, she's up on her feet, kissing Bennett, allowing him to taste my release from her mouth. I watch in awe as they share the sticky white liquid. He sucks on her tongue, her mischievous gaze on me as she taunts me once more, feeding my cum to my best friend.

"Time for dinner," she squeaks, hopping off Bennett. She spins on her heel with a giggle bubbling from her perfect mouth and runs into the bedroom. We waste no time following her because she's right, it's dinner time, and we're about to devour her sweet pussy.

THIRTY ONE

BENNETT

"YOU UNDERESTIMATE US, SWEETHEART." My voice drips thick with lust for her. She's bent over the bed before Carter and me in black lingerie. The thong fits around her waist and slips between firm, round arse cheeks I want to mark with my firm hand. To watch her back curve as I spank her has my dick throbbing. Painful. Hard. Aching.

"And how do you figure that out, Bennett?" Her cheeky retort has my palm itching to feel her skin against it. That's the only thing clouding my mind. It's a blanket of emotion that covers us in its safety net.

"Sweetheart, don't tempt me, my hand is tingling. Do you know what's making it tingle?" My growl sends a shiver over her body and I can't hide my satisfied smirk.

"You want to spank this?" She wiggles her arse and I just about come in my trousers. Fuck, this woman will be my end. Her gray gaze peeks at me over her shoulder. My little lioness, with her sights set on her dinner, and we're fucked because I know my best friend will help me devour her right here.

Leaning forward, I grip her arse cheeks and squeeze. They're so smooth, supple, and I want to spank her. But I don't. I tease her by massaging them in slow circles. Carter moves toward her mouth, his lips on hers as he kisses her savagely. Her whimpers are a chorus of beautiful notes.

I move back but command her, "Stay."

And she does. Her sweetly submissive side is sexy as fuck and when she pouts it takes all my fucking restraint not to forget where I am and fuck her mercilessly.

"Carter, I think our little tease wants to watch for a little longer. Come here," I tell him, shoving my boxers down my thighs. She quickly moves onto her back, against the headboard. Tentatively, she spreads her thighs, her fingers delving between those puffy lips of her pussy as she taunts us.

"Time to play, sweetheart," I tell her, dropping to my knees. I take Carter's dick in my mouth. Her gasp is enough to spur me on as he slowly hardens again. I don't look at her but merely taunt my best friend, tasting him as I fist my own rock-hard erection.

Once he's solid steel in my mouth, I release him with a pop.

"Fuck her pretty pussy. I want to taste her juices all over you," I tell him.

He nods and I watch as he crawls over to her. The knickers she's been wearing are gone with one hard tug. Material whooshes to the floor as I take my position at her mouth. I'm so close to orgasm, I know watching him fuck her will do me in.

He slips into her tight heat, inch by inch, causing her to gasp around my shaft. "Princess, you're so fucking perfect." His hoarse growl is evidence that he's about to lose it and I can't help grinning like a fucking idiot. This is my life. The two people I love more than anything.

There's nothing about that woman that should change. And she's ours now.

"Sweetheart, I want you to drench his cock," I tell her.

She attempts a nod, but it's not working. Her mouth his full of my cock, and her tight little hole is swallowing Carter's dick.

We move in sync, the three of us. The heat in the room is unbearable as we tease, taunt, and lick each other. My mouth is on Carter's as he ploughs into Ella's pussy. The sounds of sex are a symphony of pleasure. Her whimpers come harder, faster, and I realize she's close. Leaning in, I circle her clit with my finger as Carter's hands grip her hips.

Her scream is muffled by my cock and that sets me off. I release jet after jet of cum in her mouth, coating her tongue. Three bodies tremble and shudder as pleasure races through us. We're all connected. There's no denying this is what we need.

I slip from her mouth as Carter moves away from her, allowing me to lick and lave at his softening shaft. Her flavor mixed with his is a heady mixture and I savor every drop. I find myself settling between her legs, my mouth suckling on her smooth lips, tasting the hot seed dripping from her delicious pussy.

"I want to eat this sweet little cunt until you're squirting all over my face," I tell her.

Her eyes find mine and she watches in awe as my mouth devours her.

This woman turns me on to no end when she arches her back as pleasure rockets through her like a storm raging wildly. Being between her legs is the gasoline to my fire. Stoking it, teasing it. Making it flare with need.

My eyes dart between Carter and Ella, both watching me. Her tiny hand reaches for him, looking at him, then me.

"I want more," she mumbles.

He looks at me then nods. Her body is still trembling when I move over and lie beside her. We position her over my cock, while Carter, who's about to lick her from behind, prowls toward the end of the bed. She slips down gently, easing herself onto my erection.

My best friend disappears, his mouth already feasting on her. His tongue laps at her and me as we fuck slow and steady. Her lips part in whimpering moans that heat my blood.

"I need it." Her words are a soft plea and she knows she doesn't need to ask me twice. I lift my hips as she comes down on my cock. I'm pistoning into her, fucking her hard. "Yes," she cries out. Her concentration falters when Carter drives two fingers inside her arse, which has her screeching our names.

"Fuck, Ella," I growl and her beautiful face is flushed. Her eyes are shining with love, lust, and desire. "Fuck my dick, baby. I want you to drench me. I want to feel you pulse around my thick cock while Cart eats your holes." My body is humming, vibrating with raw, primal need to take this woman and own every fucking beautiful inch of her.

Her soft rosy lips open. They crash down on mine in a searing kiss. Our tongues dance, our bodies connect. I grip the sheets so hard I'm sure I'm about to rip through the material. The warmth of her mouth and the way her cunt sucks me in have my balls tightening.

She takes me like a woman who's possessed. It's then that Carter must fuck his fingers into her because her moan is loud even though my tongue is deep inside her mouth. My body spasms and her eyes lock on mine. He does it again and again as he licks and tastes her.

"Come for us, sweetheart," I growl as she whimpers my name, which sends me spiraling into infinite darkness. My body locks and jet after jet of hot cum shoots inside her.

It takes a moment for my vision to clear from the orgasm. When I glance down I find my beautiful woman sharing my dick with my best friend as they both lick me clean.

"That was fun." Her honeyed, raspy tone has me smirking. There's nothing innocent about her.

I glance at my best friend, whose chin is glistening with our juices.

"Come here, Princess," Carter murmurs. He leans up, tugging her to him, and their lips touch lightly. "Taste your sweetness on me."

Her tongue flicks out, lapping at the arousal that's coated on his lips. The act itself is erotic and sensual. Her beautiful back arched and her arse sticking out make me want to rush this, but I don't. A drink first, then we can play. I need to recover from that mind-blowing orgasm.

"I'm getting some drinks," I inform them with a chuckle. Heading to the bar, I pour three shots of whisky and pick up the tumblers. When I return to the bedroom, they're lounging on the bed, with space for me on the other side of our girl.

I hand them each a glass. "To us," I toast and we clink our tumblers. I down mine in one long gulp, enjoying the burn of the alcohol. "Play with your pussy, Princess. Let me see you," I order.

She swallows the strong liquid and winces as she finishes it in one draw. Then she leans back on the bed, her legs part, and her slender fingers stroke her bare lips.

They're glistening with her earlier orgasm, including mine and Carter's arousal inside her. A pretty cream pie. The pulse in my dick throbs and I harden, ready for round two. Carter's gaze is locked on her movements and his hand drops to his already hardening dick, stroking it as he watches her fingers dip into the tight heat of her drenched center.

EPILOGUE

BENNETT

"**W**HERE ARE WE GOING?" ELLA QUESTIONS FOR the hundredth time.

Carter and I have signed the paperwork for the house. It's in our name. All three of us. Soon we'll join as a family.

Ella will take both our last names. She had said she didn't want marriage and a ceremony, but soon she'll wear both our rings. We've decided to get something that will interlock on her left hand so that assholes know she's taken.

When I pull up the drive, I notice Carter's already here. He's at the door, waiting. I turn off the engine and exit the vehicle. When I finally help Ella from the car, she's sighing. I know she's frustrated, which only makes this even more fun.

We head up to the door where Carter stands to her left and I'm on her right. The blindfold I ensured was in place still hides the beautiful house we've bought. Two floors, open brick face with white pillars on either side of the door. There are shrubs of orange blossom, lavender, and mint that are planted on either side of the entrance.

Being just outside the city, it's quiet with good schools in the area. We're hoping for two beautiful babies. One of mine and one of Carter's. A perfect family.

"Can you please tell me what we're doing?" Ella huffs petulantly, causing me to chuckle. Carter pulls her blindfold off. We watch her blink a few times, and I know she's trying to figure out what the hell we're doing.

"Welcome home, sweetheart," I tell her.

"This is where we'll make our new memories," Carter informs her in a low whisper.

"Are you... Are you serious?" Her smile is so bright, the sun doesn't need to shine because she's the only warmth we need. She races to the door, shoving the large wooden door open.

"I think we did good," I tell my best friend.

"We always do good." He winks as we follow our girl into our new home.

ELLA

My body feels weightless, as if I'm floating on water. They both make me feel beautiful, sensual, wanted. Carter walks over to me. He's rock hard and I know I'm about to find euphoria. I realize they're both deeply ingrained in my soul.

Both men fought for me. They both love me in their own way.

"Come here, Princess." Carter lifts me up and we head into the bedroom. I feel the heat of his best friend behind me and the safety I've always felt with them blankets me.

My head is already spinning, intoxicated by them. Every nerve in my body thrums with delight, with need, with desire. Carter places me on the bed and flops down beside me. Bennett joins us and I'm once again sandwiched between my two princes.

They slayed the dragon and here I am, being worshipped like a queen. And that's what they make me feel, cherished. Each man strokes my body tenderly, lovingly. My skin ignites as lust takes over, licking its way over my bare flesh.

"So beautiful," Bennett whispers in my ear.

Carter's lips find the sensitive skin on my neck and he kisses his way down to my pebbled nipple, suckling one, causing me to shiver with desire.

Another mouth, equally as warm, envelops the other and I'm flying. Soaring so high I don't think I'll ever want to come down. My back arches and they both graze my sensitive buds with their teeth, sending my body reeling. I'm wet. I'm needy.

Fingers tease their way down, dipping into my belly button and then lowering to where I need them. A soft touch teases my core, stroking my sex and then dipping into the slick lips of my pussy. One finger. Two fingers. Euphoria as they both bite down on my nipples and I find a release, my body dripping lust onto the fingers that explore me.

"God, oh, yes, please." Words fall from my lips. None of them make sense, but they're vocalized by me. My eyes flutter closed and I inhale a deep, calming breath as the scent of them mixes with the heavy fog of sex that hangs above us like a curtain, cloaking us from the world outside.

Mouths move, hands stroke, and fingers explore. I'm mindless, consumed, needy in its basest form. The feral need for release, for an orgasm overwhelms me.

"That's my girl. Come for me. I want to taste you."

I don't know who it is, which of the two men coaxes me, but I feel his mouth lapping at me. Sucking my clit into his mouth and biting down as his finger pumps deep into me, my toes curl and before I can fall another mouth swallows my whimpers as his tongue darts into my mouth, devouring me.

"Come for me, Princess." It's Carter. His voice is a husky growl as he commands my body to topple and I do.

My thighs clench around his head as he crooks his fingers and an orgasm that's mind-numbing and earth-shattering courses through my blood and ignites my veins. I cry out, but Bennett ravishes me and his tongue swipes along mine, claiming my sounds of ecstasy.

When he finally breaks away, I'm lifted and Carter settles on the bed, his gaze molten blue. "Sit on my cock, baby. I need to feel you."

I do. My body moves and I straddle him. He grips his thick shaft and as I sink on his cock my body stretches.

"Carter, fuck."

A wicked smirk curls his lips. "That's what I intend doing, Princess." Gripping my hips, he pulls me down on him, impaling me with his dick. Bennett's hands stroke my back as he feathers kisses down my spine. "Come here."

I lean over Carter, offering myself to the man behind me. His fingers knead my ass, massaging each cheek until I'm once again humming with desire.

A snap of a plastic tube echoes in the room and then I feel the cold liquid drenching my puckered hole. "So pretty, sweetheart." Bennett growls as his fingers tease and taunt the tight ring of muscle. He eases one finger in, slowly pumping it, then I feel the second digit. He scissors me open, loosening me up so I can take his hard erection.

Even though his fingers are no match for his cock, I relax at the sensations racing through me.

"Our naughty girl. She loves two men taking her. Don't you, baby?" Carter's words have me grinning and I nod. His mouth finds my nipple once more, while his hand teases the other. They're taut and sensitive to his touch.

My mind is racing, reeling, then I feel it. Bennett's

intrusion has me crying out his name and my nails dig into Carter's shoulders. He moves slowly, sinking into me.

"Sweet Lord, you're so fucking tight." When he's fully seated, I'm filled. Completely. Without a doubt, my body is at its peak. Both my saviors start moving, in and out in a torturously slow rhythm that has my skin prickling.

"Look at me, Princess," the man below me murmurs into my ear and I snap my gaze to his. Those normally blue eyes are dark and sinful. Filled with need.

I've given them my all.

My heart. My body. My soul.

Soft strokes down my spine send shivers trickling through me and I tense. Both men gasp and I feel powerful. I control them. Their pleasure, their bodies.

"I can't…" I whimper. I don't want them to stop, but I don't know if I can hold on much longer.

"Ella, look at me." Dragging my eyes to Bennett's, I latch onto his gaze. "You're going to come. You're going to come all over our cocks. Give us every fucking ounce of pleasure you have." He reaches down between us and pinches my clit so hard I shriek, but it's not pain causing me to cry out, it's the overwhelming pleasure that shatters me.

And I do. In that moment, I give two men everything. My body tenses, and they both groan. I feel them thicken and their pace increases.

"I'm going to fill this tight little arse, sweetheart." And he does. Jet after jet of warm release shoots into me and I shudder again. Blinding light seeps into my vision.

"This is my sweet girl, Princess." Carter's rumbled words vibrate through me and the last thing I remember is feeling him shoot his cum inside me, deep into my womb.

CARTER

I've got everything planned, but my heart is racing at a million miles a second. *Is that normal?* She should be home from work soon and I know as soon as she walks in everything is going to change. There have been so many dark moments. Days where I never thought we'd make it this far, but we have.

The candles are lit all around the dining room and I have the champagne on ice. The fire is roaring and I plan on making love to her on every surface I can find tonight. When I hear the car pulling up to the entrance, I nod at Bennett, who's at the table. I push up from the chair and head to the door to meet her.

When she steps inside, I notice her hair is falling loose from the black clip that's keeping the rest in a messy bun.

"Hello, Princess," I murmur, tugging her into my embrace. Her body molds to mine. The scent of her orange blossom perfume mingled with coffee and chocolate makes me chuckle.

"What?" She pulls away, pouting at me.

"You smell like chocolate," I respond before placing a soft kiss on her lips.

She giggles and the sound fills my heart with emotion akin to being high. Or drunk. Something that people pay thousands of pounds for. But here I have it in my arms and it's free.

"I had chocolate cake at the office. I'm eating for two, you know."

Shaking my head at her insistence, I lace my fingers through hers. "I know," I appease her.

We found out she's pregnant. We don't know who's the father yet. We've both kept her sated and it could be mine or Bennett's, but we don't care. This is our family now.

"You do realize that eating for two doesn't mean you have to finish all the cake," I tease her.

Another sweet, soft giggle escapes her as she pulls free, slapping me on the arm.

"Stop being such a spoil sport. It was delicious."

As soon as we walk into the dining room she gasps. The dimly lit area is romantic and it's perfect for what we have in mind.

"I've planned dinner and I need to talk to you about something else as well. So please get your sexy arse on the chair," I order, watching Bennett pull out the one right at the head of the table. The need to shock her, leaving her speechless is one of my favorite things to do, because I know she'll play right into my hands.

When she finally settles, I take in her appearance. Her body is perfect as she grows with our baby. Her eyes are glistening with happiness. Both Bennett and I take our seat on either side of her.

"What did you want to talk about?" she asks, running her fingers through her long blond hair.

She's perfection in its purest form and I know I'll never get my heart back because this woman has consumed every fiber of my being.

Pulling the champagne from the ice bucket, I unwrap the foil and pop the cork. Grabbing two crystal flutes, I fill them with sparkling golden liquid. I've made sure it's free of alcohol so she isn't drinking while being pregnant.

"There's something we need to celebrate."

She cocks her head to the side, regarding me and my best friend as I hand her the glass. It's warm outside and the moon lights her in its blue light, making her ethereal. Like an angel. Sweet and beautiful. Innocent, yet not.

It hurts me to know what she endured. What vile things her life has shown her, but when I look at her now, the strength she's shown has given me the courage to do this.

It's allowed me to see the heart of who I am, and what I want. Our dinner is on the table, ready to be devoured, but I wonder if she'll see the surprise before I have a chance to ask her. I never planned it, but when I spoke to Bennett, he gave me the go ahead. The reasoning is simple. I love her, but I also want our child to know that even though there are two men who are father figures, that legally, she isn't a single mother.

"What are we celebrating?" she questions quietly.

"There've been many times over these few months that I've wondered why you're still here. We're not the easiest men to put up with, but when we almost lost you something in me shifted. There was always a connection between us, but something hit me the day we found you. The idea of losing you cut into me like a blade slicing through my still beating heart." I push up off the chair and position myself in front of her. "I spoke to Bennett and we've agreed that I should be the one to do this. You've embedded yourself in our minds, and even though you have us both here, loving you, wanting you, giving you all you need. My soul needs yours to survive, Princess. I need you. So, I'd like to ask if you'd perhaps want to make it legal?"

"I agree. I want this for you both. I'm not going anywhere. Don't take this the wrong way. But you need a legal husband to ensure our children are safe. And I can't think of a better man than Carter."

She glances between us. Her face is a picture of elation and shock. I pull out the ring Bennett and I bought her. It's two rings, for both of us, twined into one. Since only one of us can marry her, it's a symbol of both our love for her.

"Of course, yes, yes," she mumbles through tears. She pulls us both into her embrace and I know this is my happily ever after.

PLAYLIST

THE MUSIC

- Tainted Love - Marilyn Manson
- Sweet Dreams - Emily Browning
- Desire - Meg Myers
- Bad Girl - Avril Lavigne & Marilyn Manson
- Sick Like Me - In This Moment
- Dark in my Imagination - of Verona
- Dangerous Woman - Ariana Grande
- Monster - Meg Myers
- You Don't Own Me - Grace & G-Eazy
- Cold Sweats - BLKNZ & SATICA
  Find the playlist on Spotify

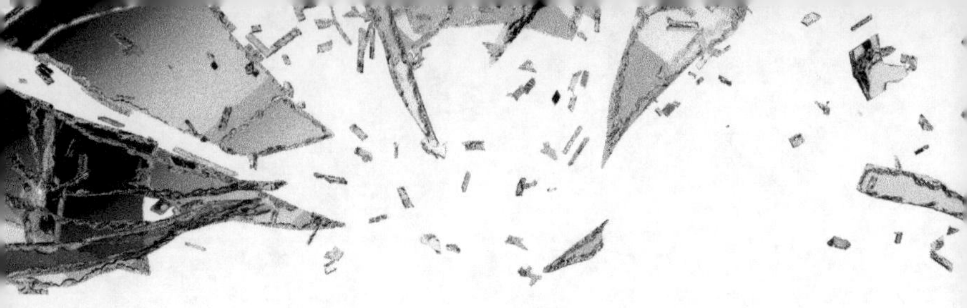

THANK YOU

ACKNOWLEDGMENTS

I started this story in 2016 as part of a series I was planning, but something felt wrong. it wasn't working. I put it on the back burner and late last year, Carter and Bennett started shouting at me. Ella then pushed me into the cave and told me her story.

It was difficult to write at certain points. Some of the scenes made me cringe, brought tears to my eyes, but I needed to write it. And in the end, I fell in love with these three.

I need to thank my BETAs, for taking a chance on this story with me. I know most of you will never look at a snow globe the same way again, and I apologize for that. But you stuck by me and even fought over who was claiming Carter and who wanted Bennett. You loved Ella's strength and that to me meant everything. Thank you, Sheena, Melissa, Cat, Caroline, Joy, Amy, and Allyson for everything!

To the amazing Emily Lawrence, of Lawrence Editing for taking my story and polishing it. Your input is appreciated. I can't thank you enough for everything.

My Decadent Dolls street team, thank you for pimping my work EVERYWHERE. You ladies rock!!

My reader group, Dani's Darklings, thank you for being a place for me to escape the craziness and just have a laugh. And thank you for all the support for my books and loving my alphas.

To all my author colleagues, thank you for always sharing, commenting, and supporting me. I appreciate every one of you. Having a support system is important and you ladies provide that and so much more.

Readers and bloggers, from the bottom of my little black heart, THANK YOU. All you do for us authors is incredible. Reading and reviewing is demanding on your own time and you do it with a smile. Thank you so, so much. You are valued and appreciated for taking time out to show us so much love.

If you enjoyed this story, please consider leaving a review. I'd love you forever. (Even though I already do!)

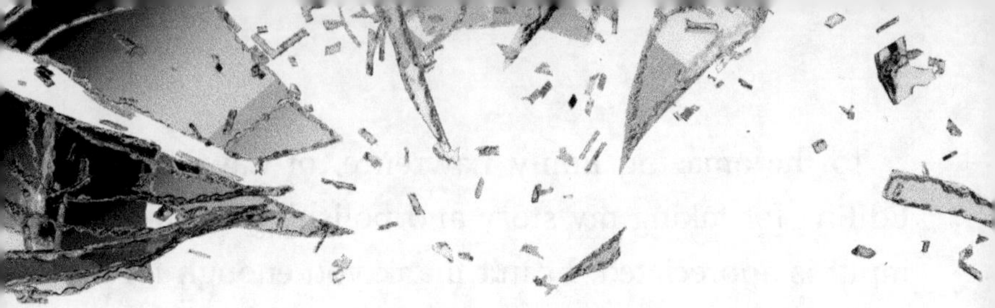

ABOUT

THE AUTHOR

Dani is a USA Today Bestselling Author of dark and deviant romance with a seductive edge.

Originally from Cape Town, South Africa, she now lives in the UK with her better half who does all the cooking while she writes all the words. When she's not writing, she can be found binge-watching the latest TV series, or working on graphic design either for herself, or other indie authors. She enjoys reading books about handsome villains and feisty heroines, mostly dark, always seductive, and sometimes depraved. She has a healthy addiction to tattoos, coffee, and ice cream.

www.danirene.com

info@danirene.com

FIND ME ONLINE

STALK LINKS

Do you follow me?

If not, head over to any of the below sites,

I love to hear from my readers!

Amazon - http://bit.ly/DaniAmazon

BookBub - http://bit.ly/DaniBookBub

Facebook - http://bit.ly/DaniFBPage

Facebook Group - Dani's Deviants

Goodreads - http://bit.ly/DaniGoodreads

Twitter - @danireneauthor

Pinterest - @danireneauthor

Instagram - @danireneauthor

Spotify - http://bit.ly/DaniSpotify

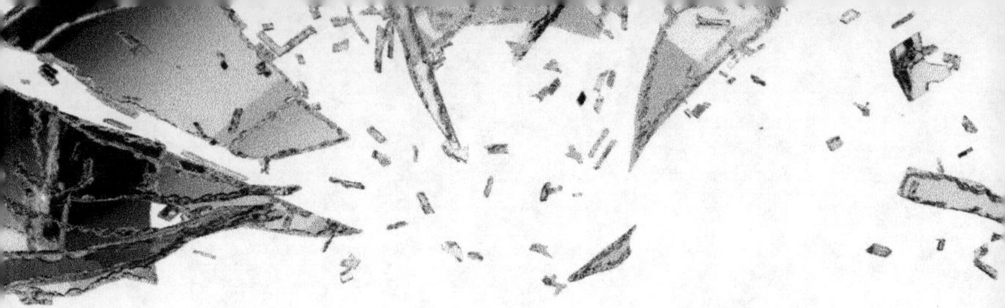

OTHER BOOKS

BY THE AUTHOR

<u>Stand Alones</u>

Choosing the Hart

Love Beyond Words

Cuffed

Fragile Innocence

Perfectly Flawed

Black Light: Obsessed

Among Ash and Ember

Within Me (Limited Time)

Cursed in Love (collaboration with Cora Kenborn)

Beautifully Brutal (Cavalieri Della Morte)

How the Mind Breaks

The Devil's Plaything

While She Sleeps (Dirty Heroes Collection)

It's Never Easy (Lady Boss Press)

Only One Night (Lady Boss Press)

Deviant (Black Mountain Academy)

<u>Taboo Novellas</u>

Sunshine and the Stalker (collab. with K Webster)

His Temptation

Austin's Christmas Shortcake

Crime and Punishment (Newsletter Exclusive)

Malignus (Inferno World Novella)

Tempting Grayson

<u>Gilded Sovereign Series</u>

Cruel War (Book #1)

Volatile Love (Book #2)

<u>Sins of Seven Series</u>

Kneel (Book #1)

Obey (Book #2)

Indulge (Book #3)

Ruthless (Book #4)

Bound (Book #5)

Envy (Book #6)

Vice (Book #7)

<u>The Taken Series</u>

Stolen

Severed

<u>Four Fathers Series</u>

Kingston

<u>Four Sons Series</u>

Brock

<u>Carina Press Novellas</u>

Pierced Ink

Madd Ink

<u>Broken Series</u>

Broken by Desire

Shattered by Love

<u>The Backstage Series</u>

Callum

Liam

Ryan

<u>Forbidden Series</u>

From the Ashes - A Prequel

Crave (Book #1)

Covet (Book #2)